The
COURT

PALMETTO
PUBLISHING
Charleston, SC
www.PalmettoPublishing.com

Copyright © 2024 by Will Sutter

All rights reserved
No portion of this book may be reproduced, stored in a retrieval system, or transmitted in any form by any means—electronic, mechanical, photocopy, recording, or other—except for brief quotations in printed reviews, without prior permission of the author.

Paperback ISBN: 979-8-8229-4460-2

WILL SUTTER

The
COURT

CHAPTER ONE

The gently swelling land between Sugar Loaf Mountain and the Potomac is dimpled with farms and small woods and cut here and there by little ravines where streams race for the river.

I bicycle the country several times a week. Sometimes I take a stretch on the old C & O Canal for the river views.

The country is well mixed with history. Union cavalry patrolled it during the Civil War, and Lee and his army traversed the country on his way to defeat at Antietam. Jeb Stuart used it as a playground for his cavalry during the Gettysburg campaign.

All this made it the perfect place to live when I was able to work from home. I like a nice landscape with at least a bit of a past. Carol McAdams lives in Jimtown on a street featuring some lovely Victorians that lift it above a typical village. Carol has one of those. I live in a refurbished farmhouse on a fair piece of ground. Sugar Loaf is about a mile away and clearly visible from my front porch. I rent out the ground to a local farmer who in turn takes care of the property. Carol and I spend several hours a week together and sometime sleep over, me at hers and she at mine. It's an arrangement that suits us both.

    Jim Main, my editor at the Washington Standard, wants me to do opinion pieces on the Supreme Court. The occasion is the upcoming hearings on the nomination of Jessup McDowell as chief justice of the Supreme Court. McDowell is a flaming conservative who believes the Court is the leading institution of our government, the constitutional conscience of the nation saying what the government can and can't do for the People. Many think it an extreme view, unconstitutional even. Jim and I are among them. Since the Standard is the most read paper in our halls of power, what Jim and I have to say on the matter will have some swing. Makes me feel like a knight of old answering the bugle's call.

CHAPTER TWO

I first saw Carol sitting by herself in Patty's Patio, an overly cute name for a small café in Jimtown. It's the favorite meeting place for people like us, mid and upper-level white collars, heretofore confined in our Washington offices like so many bovines in their pasture, freed now by Covid and the internet. We are spread around Washington on both sides of the Potomac in a spackled pattern. I wanted to meet her. She looked to be at first glance a member in good standing of the Docker crowd, enjoying their Mocha and munchy. But there was something different, too, in her face. She was there with them but not totally of them. It was that different I wanted to know. She was knitting something, a scarf it looked like.

I walked up to her table and said, "If you're not booked up, can I order a sweater when you're done?"

She chuckled. "It's for a friend," she said, an ambiguous answer.

"Lucky him," I said.

"It's a she," she said with a grin, knowing what I was at, the grin saying she wasn't put off.

"This chair taken?"

"No," she said, the friendly grin still in place.

"I'm Carl," I said.

"Carol," she said. "Carl what?"

"Carl Schulz."

The friendly grin changed to friendly interest.

"The journalist with the Standard?"

"Guilty," I said. "You know about me?"

"I read the Standard," she said.

"I'm flattered," I said.

She shrugged. "People say I should meet you."

"Flattered again," I said. "I didn't realize I had allies working on my behalf."

"I'm a lawyer," she said. "I work with law firms arguing before the Court. I help them with their briefs. It's my specialty. You guys are about to weigh in on the McDowell hearings, and not in a supportive way, I suspect. I would have an interest."

It went on from there. Despite my initial fears, she was not necessarily a friend of the Court when it came to judicial review, the pretension of federal judges to be the definitive readers of the Constitution. As she later explained to me, "The court applying federal law to the federation is one thing. The courts telling the Congress, the president or the voters how to read the Constitution is something else. Is the Constitution a user's guide to the government and its powers available to all to interpret or is it a sacred text comprehensible only to the judges?"

THE COURT

It was one more nice thing added to the already nice things happening to us.

I ride for a couple of hours four times a week. This countryside is made for bicyclists like me, some strenuous exercise but no where near the Tour de France level. My style is rolling through open fields spotted here and there by distant farmhouses and whizzing down a ravine's tunnel of dark green tunnel foliage, at the bottom a stream waiting, purling over its rocky bed to the Potomac. The stream's coolness is Dame Nature's reward for enduring the heat of her simmering fields, keeping the balance.

McDowell calls the Court America's constitutional conscience, typical of the smug self-satisfaction of many of these judges. The Constitution calls for this?

CHAPTER THREE

Our first get together was to a movie in nearby Frederick. When I suggested it, she said she would meet me there. "Why not go in one car?" I replied. "We can talk on the way." That was agreeable.

"You make a living writing briefs?" I asked, passing Sugar Loaf with some small farms between the road and the loaf shaped mountain's point of lift off.

"It's steady and solid," she said, "and payed the bills. Not lucrative, maybe, but I had lucrative when I was a partner with Burlings and Bishop. With my cash out and an inheritance from my father I'm OK."

The BBs, I note, what Burlings and Bishop is called in Washington's corridors of power, is a blue-chip firm with a big foot in lobbying and another one representing top government officials caught in some partisan food fight on the Hill.

"You?" she said. "You work from home now?"

THE COURT

"Mostly. I usually go in once a week. I came out here because of Covid, also a little tired of the daily city hassle. Twenty years was enough, even with the break in Rome as bureau chief. I do miss the newsroom. It has at certain smell and bustle that has a home like comfort after so many years. I need a bit of it every week. I also like keeping in touch with folks on the Hill and the White House. Viewing from a remove gives a certain perspective, but you need face to face to get a real feel for things."

She nodded. "I can see that," she said, "if you are writing about contemporary events. My law books and the internet do it for me. I love glancing out my study window to see my garden as I organize my research for a brief. Dried facts aren't as slippery as people."

I looked over to see if she was joking. Apparently not.

"A good scholar," I ventured.

"I've been told that," she said. "Regard it as a compliment. But I'm also a good lawyer."

No lack of confidence there. "So why'd you leave?" I asked, curious.

Some say I'm too forward. I'm a journalist. Journalists find things out. You don't do that unless you ask a lot questions, forward or not.

"I was good at what I did and I enjoyed the game, the competition, the legal combat, but it got to where each new case was just a variation of the one before. I had enough. I needed something new, stimulating, still, but new."

"Describes me, too. I loved reporting, digging out the facts, making a story."

"So why'd you turn to punditry?"

This was comfortable, talking like real friends, no need to feint and dodge, strangers sniffing each other out, making harmless chit chat. It suggested a promising future. I'd like that, I thought, giving a quick glance at her tawny mane with just a hint of gray.

"Well, it's still reporting, gathering the facts and writing a good narrative, but now I get to add my opinion. Still a reporter, just an opinionated one.

She chuckled. "You're certainly that."

"You read my stuff?"

"All the time," she said.

"And?"

She looked at me. "You want a critique?"

"A modest appreciation will do," I said.

Another laugh. "Usually you provoke a good argument."

"OK," I said tapping the wheel, "have at it."

"Why don't we enjoy the movie first. Time later for a good talk."

"Look forward to it," I said.

I was taking a country road parallel to Interstate 495 which links Frederick to Washington. I like the countryside route, the farms, the isolated homes, fields and woods all around, on the way to red brick Frederick, a fun time rather than just getting there. The countryside left to itself has a lot to say. Carol seemed to get it. She sat there gazing out the window with a happy smile.

The movie was No Country for Old Men, a film version of Cormac McCarthy's novel of the same name. It was a release of many years earlier enjoying now a revival following the author's death. I was in Rome at the time of its release. Carol hadn't seen it either, totally absorbed at the time in some case involving testimony on the Hill. For both of us it was a premiere.

McCarthy was a good writer, though his mixture of tenderness and violence is not to everyone's taste. After the film, we indulged in an ice cream from a shop on the plaza next to the movie theater. It sold high end ice cream, gelato, one of Italy's incomparable contributions to the field, a speciality. If it wasn't the mother of all ice creams, it was certainly the most glorious of its ancestors. As soon as I saw the sign, I told Carol, "You've got to try this."

"Heard of it," she said, "but never had it. This is a first."

As we were licking our way through our gelato she visibly shuddered.

"You don't like it?" I asked, mildly alarmed. I was hoping the gelato would help make my case with her.

"I do," she said to my relief. "I was thinking of the movie. Imagine killing someone with a bolt gun, what they use to put down cows for butchering." She shuddered again. "He does have an imagination," she said, emphasizing does.

"You think the violence is over the top?"

She shrugged. "It's part of life. Killers use some vicious tools. Perverse, but part of human nature. Twentieth century history is textbook."

"The question is, metaphor, or is he just wallowing in the moral mud?"

She laughed. "One of the things I notice about your pieces, the odd but apt turn of phrase." She looked at me, inviting more, flattering. She was genuinely interested, I felt, no pretense. She didn't seem do things just for forms' sake.

"Maybe another way to put it, he believes violence is endemic in humans, a point he wants to dramatize rather than just sensationalize?"

She laughed. "All this over gelato? What happens when it's a full-fledged Italian meal."

"It's not the ice cream," I said, "It's you."

There was a nice change to her eyes.

CHAPTER FOUR

"The constitutional conscience of the nation. Is that what is meant by 'The judicial power of the United States shall be vested in one supreme court, and in such inferior Courts as the Congress may... establish'?" I wrote. "Nothing in that says a court can overturn a law passed by Congress and signed by the President.

"A proposal becomes law when it has '...passed the House of Representatives and the Senate...' and is '...presented to the President of the United States...' for his signature. This is how Article l, section 7 of the Constitution describes the process. There is no mention of the Supreme Court. The president with his veto pen and the electorate with their votes are the only two parties with the explicit Constitutional power to change what Congress does. What is Jessup McDowell's authority for claiming the Court is the conscience of the government?"

My rides along the C&O Canal are special. No hills, for one thing, easier pedaling. But there's a drawback. Though the tow path is flat, after a bit you begin imagining resistance, like a hill. It's not really there, but you still feel it. A hill you can see and make the adjustment. The tow path sneaks up on you. Apart from that, riding it is a pleasure.

It took some effort to build that 184-mile watercourse linking sea level Georgetown to Cumberland, Maryland, tucked away in the Appalachians, 605 feet above sea level. Between the two points the Potomac enjoys level stretches which could be navigated, but at other points it tumbles over rapids on its descent from the mountains. If you want to enjoy the ease of travel by this water path, you need a Canal.

As I passed the ruins of the canal locks, some of them still intact enough to resemble their original selves, I reflected on how they leveled out the tumbling river. When the canal reaches a point where the river falls even a few feet, it either stops or finds a way of lifting itself to the new level. Barges are too heavy to be carried to smooth water the way French voyagers carried their canoes around rapids, portaging, they called it.

Stopping to look at one of these roughhewn marvels, I imagined a bunch of Irish pick men, all jabbering in a version of English natives found hard to follow, and the civil engineers, some graduates of the United States Military Academy at West Point, with their set of rudimentary surveying instruments, all staring at the problem.

The motley crew set to digging a rectangular pit long enough to hold a forty-foot barge. They affixed large doors at either end that could be swung open, a modest sized portal at the bottom of each to admit and release water, filling or emptying the lock.

When our barge from Georgetown reaches this first ascent of the river, the bargeman blows a horn to let the gate keeper know he's approaching. The gate keeper opens the lower gate doors and lets the barge in. He then shut the door and opens the small port of the upper door to fill the rectangular lock, lifting the barge as it fills. The upper door is then swung open, and the barge, raised by the magical power of water, goes on its merry way. The process is reversed for barges coming down from Cumberland.

By this process, not invented by them but fruitfully applied by the canal builders, tons of rock, coal and so many other products of the hinterland moved almost effortlessly to Georgetown, satisfying the capital's ravenous appetite for building materials. Some of it was also shipped to ports along the East Coast or to foreign destinations. Before the canal, those things had to come to Washington by way if horse and wagon, slow, expensive, laborious and tough on the horses.

I imagined the bargeman jumping ashore and approaching the lock keeper to chat, eager for whatever news, gossip or stories might be on tap. The gatekeeper, too, would certainly want to know what was going on in Washington City, what the president was up to, any tellings about members of Congress, especially local representatives or Maryland's two senators, what the men about town were wearing, any juicy murders, anything the gate keeper could pass on to family or neighbors. When finished, the bargeman would wait expectantly for the reverse flow of what events were roiling the local waters, romances, family feuds, local government outrages, crop information, all eagerly provided and eagerly received. The canal was more than a conduit for commerce, it was also a conduit for news big and small running up and down its one hundred eighty-four-mile length like crackling electricity. The canal was in effect the watery line of communications of a mini society linking towns and villages up and down its length.

That day I planned to ride as far as the railroad bridge over the river to Harper's Ferry, another one of the Potomac's nodules of history.

Back in the day, it was mules, not bicyclists or day hikers, on the graveled tow path, two of them tugging the barge gently along. When not working, they rested and fed in a small enclosure on the front of the barge. The barge man lived in quarters at the opposite end along with any family accompanying him. I imagined these limited quarters also furnished the scene for many a canal tryst.

Now most of this once thriving aquatic highway is a tree choked shallow depression in the ground marked periodically by the ruined stone lined locks, sad reminders of this once living aquatic passage connecting tide water America with its mountainous interior.

And more than the canal had changed from that rural, technologically primitive America of the past to what we see today. The Court, too, I thought as I pedaled, had changed in the way it saw the Constitution.

Before the Civil War the Court applied the Constitution and federal law to the subordinate states, defining and clarifying the federal relationship while steering clear of "policy" questions, as Marshall called therm. Those were the business of Congress.

For instance, when the New York legislature in 1803 granted a monopoly to a Manhattan steam boat company, co-founded by Robert Fulton, father of the steam boat, to conduct ferry service between Manhattan and New Jersey, the Court said no: the regulation of commerce between states belonged to Congress, not the states. By this decision, the Supreme Court opened the Hudson to a richer, more varied commerce than allowed by the crabbed model supplied by the New York state Legislature. It was a win for the nation.

In the view of the Court, the Constitution was a living, breathing political document, well suited to the needs of a growing, changing nation, not a rigid, meaning-set-for-ever statue, mysteries open only to a handful of élite judges. Some years later, another suit tried to stop Pennsylvania from requiring all river traffic on the Delaware, except local, to have a river pilot, necessary for navigational safety.

It was challenged. Only Congress could regulate inter state commerce, the challengers said. The Court disagreed. The river traffic essentially affected only Pennsylvania and its close neighbors, presumably in agreement, not the nation at large, making it essentially a local matter not a federal one, open to state regulation. This was flexible, non-dogmatic and helpful to the common good, political pragmatism, not judicial philosophy, the ruling element.

But the Court was quick to protect federal prerogatives when threatened. When Maryland laid a tax on the Baltimore branch of the Bank of the United States, the Court stepped in to say no. Its 1819 decision McCulloch v Maryland said the power to tax was the power to destroy, and it was improper for a subordinate to enjoy such a power over the superior, the federal government. This was firmly rooted in Article 1, section 8 of the Constitution.

What the court of Marshall did not do was pass on the wisdom of these acts on the basis of some judicially imagined Constitutional right.

CHAPTER FIVE

"You like baseball?" Carol asked. We were becoming an item, though not clear yet what kind. It was still early. I was now going more often to Patty's hoping she'd be there, but free to sit rather than wait to be invited. She had the usual knitting going.

"You jerking my chain or what? Of course I like baseball. I played on my high school team."

'I thought so," she said, "You have that look. My law firm has several season box seat tickets. They'll let me have any that aren't being used. Want to go to a game? We could get some seafood on the Anacostia waterfront before, make a night of it."

The Standard had its own set of tickets, but this was a far better offer. "I'd love it," I said.

What 'look' she was talking about I didn't know, or how it might have persisted into my fifties. I was glad she saw it, though.

"And I played soft ball," she said, "high school and college."

"Must have been a better ball player than me. I didn't play college ball."

The tickets were to a National game against the Atlanta Braves on a September Wednesday night. The early Autumn cool was just right for a comfortable night at the ballpark to see two good teams go at it for the National League's East division title, something riding on the game.

We drove to Shady Grove and took the Metro to Navy Yard/Ballpark, the familiar drive from Jimtown to Shady Grove and the Metro ride comforting. We both took that route in our frequent shuttles in and out of town. This was our second time out together, and the familiar ride helped over any awkward newness. She was easy company, conversation flowing, unforced.

We did have seafood at one of the upscale restaurants for which the Anacostia waterfront is famous, drawing on the riches of the Chesapeake. She had blue crabs, I had sea trout, its delicate flavor unburdened by any strong fish taste. It was one of my favorites. We agreed beforehand on separate checks, though I was old fashioned enough to be uncomfortable at that. To compensate, I insisted on springing for a nice Italian Pinot Grigio, a good compliment to sea food.

"So I'll get the popcorn at the stadium," she said, keeping things even. That's where we were.

It was a relief not to have to explain baseball, a common enough task at games with many of my other female friends. Carol knew the game as well as I did.

THE COURT

The Nats won 6 to 4, some timely hitting in the 7th inning with men on base. When those two runs turned out to be the winners, Carol dryly observed, "Good pitching doesn't always beat good hitting."

Outfield had been her position. Outfielders have to hit, or somebody else will be out there.

"Maybe the pitching just faltered?" I said, keeping it going. "It has been said 'home runs are pitched, not hit."

I forgot she is a lawyer, no statement unexamined.

"Half true," she said. "Lot of home runs come off bad pitches, but really good hitters can hit a pitcher's best. It's just the mediocre ones who can't."

"You a home run hitter when you played?"

She shook her head.

 Line drive hitter, lot of singles, doubles in the gap. Doubles were fun, a race between me and the outfielder's arm. I loved beating them."

My respect for her grew, more even than for her lawyerly attainments. I had checked with friends at the Standard. Her reputation was golden, a skilled navigator of the rocks and shoals of Hill hearings, one told me, guiding government officials safely through the dangers of partisan fire fights. They came shopping for her.

"Dirty uniform." I said.

"Huhh?"

"You uniform, always dirty from sliding so much."

She laughed. "Right. "My teammates called me dirt pile."

"You like all these changes they made in the game, the pitch clock, bigger bases, limited pick-off moves, all that?"

A lawyer, maybe also a traditionalist, more the game as Babe Ruth knew it than not?

She nodded vigorously. "Every damn one," she said emphatically. "It's a nineteenth century game and they need to keep that, the symmetry of the field, the positioning of fielders, the need for athleticism. But they don't need to play it by nineteenth century time. Watching a batter step out after every pitch to re wrap his batting gloves, scratch his crotch, spit, knock his cleats and stare off into space contemplating the next pitch is a drag we don't need. Same with pitchers circumnavigating the mound after every pitch, contemplating his verities. Likewise, throwing to first time after time. Another drag. Stopping all of that didn't detract from the essence of the game one bit. It purified it. Same with the shift. There's a reason why the fielders traditionally stand where they do. Gives the hitter a chance. Look at this crowd," she said, addressing the jury. "It's a weeknight, but this is a weekend crowd. Didn't see that a couple years ago."

I wanted to argue, but couldn't. She was right. But I had stuff to add.

"You think pitching is too dominant?"

She thought for a moment. "Where you going with this?"

"Same place you were. Essence of the game. It's man against ball, isn't it? Not man against man as in football or basketball."

She thought about that for a moment. "Yeah?"

In its early days the pitcher's job was just to put the ball in play. They threw underhand at first. The pitcher puts the ball up there so the hitter has something to swing at.

THE COURT

Hit it hard enough he might reach first base, or even beyond. There's some excitement to that, guy hitting the ball, the sound of the crack of the bat, a fielder going after it, catching it or fielding it to throw to first. Some of it is man against man, but it is also man against the ball. A strikeout, the pitcher throws it, the batter swings and misses, the catcher throws it back, repeat two more times, he's out. Everyone else is just standing around watching."

"How about bases loaded, the home team at bat, three runs down, it's two outs. A hit might tie the game or at least keep the inning alive. A strike out ends it. Excitement enough for you?"

"Yeah, it is, especially for the home team. But," I said with a little grin, "it would be even more exciting if he hit a grounder to deep shortstop, the shortstop fields it with a dramatic back hand, plants his feet, fires a seed to first, beats the runner by a half step, everyone holding their breath. The place goes wild."

She looks at me and laughs. "You never give up, do you?" She punched me lightly on the arm, like teammates. "You should have been a lawyer."

The playful tap said we had passed a certain threshold.

CHAPTER SIX

Everyone says Justice Marshall established judicial review in Marbury v Madison. As I said in a recent column, wrong. The concept of judicial review, the power of a court to judge a piece of legislation or an official act against the strictures of a written constitution, had been walking the corridors of American politics well before Marbury v Madison. And what, I asked in the same column, gave the judiciary the power to create for itself a right not explicitly given it by the Constitution? Marshall said judges say what the law means. By that rubric couldn't Washington have declared, "I say what being a commander in chief means; commanders command armies and I command ours to attack Canada?"

In fact, Marbury v Madison is a poor reed on which to lean judicial review. Jefferson referred to it as one of Marshall's "legal twistifications." It was more political theater than solid constitutional law. Law schools won't agree with this, largely out of self-interest; they want lawyers and

THE COURT

the judges at the center of our political system rather than an important adjunct to it.

Political theater? you say.

Consider this; Marshall was a Federalist as was George Washington, Alexander Hamilton and John Adams. He had been a Federalist member of the Virginia legislature, the US House of Representatives, Secretary of State under John Adams, and then Chief Justice of the Supreme Court.

The Federalist took a shellacking in the elections of 1800. Jefferson won the presidency and his Democratic-Republican Party captured both houses of Congress. Only the judiciary remained in Federalist hands, due in part to the swarm of Federalists judges Adams appointed as he left office, Marshall chief among them. At that time, the Court ranked lowest in prestige on the federal totem pole, "the least dangerous branch" in Hamilton's memorable phrase.

Marshall was looking to boost the Court's prestige by a blast of the judicial trumpet. Marbury gave him the opportunity.

Marbury was a Federalist in the District of Columbia appointed by Adams as a justice of the peace. Time ran out on the Adams administration before Marbury's commission could be delivered, and Jefferson, in a fit of anti-Federalist pique, refused to deliver it.

Marbury sued in the DC District Court, asking for a writ of mandamus ordering Secretary of State Madison, the responsible official, to give him his commission. .

Marshall used the case to deliver his rallying cry.

But a problem. He strongly suspected Jefferson would give him the political middle finger if ordered to give Marbury his commission, making Marshall's blast sound more like a pathetic bleat than a call to arms, confirming the Court's weakness. It was not the impression he was looking to make.

He needed a call Jefferson could not mute.

He moved the case from the DC Federal District Court, where it belonged, to the Supreme Court under its original jurisdiction. Marbury, Marshall stated, was a "Minister" under the terms of Article Three, Section 2, of the Constitution: "In all cases affecting Ambassadors, other public Ministers and Consuls the supreme Court shall have original jurisdiction."

Most might read "minister" to mean foreign officials on US soil. Marshall wasn't interested in arguing the point, he just needed a platform from which to sound his horn without having to give Marbury his writ of mandamus, thereby avoiding a direct confrontation with Jefferson.

Marshall said Marbury had a right to his commission, but he could not issue a writ of mandamus. The Judiciary Act of 1789, which gave the federal judiciary power to issue such writs, did not apply to the Court in its original jurisdiction. What the Constitution withheld, Marshall argued, the Congress could not confer. He then uttered the words on which the power of judicial review hangs: it is the judges place to say what the Constitution means and declare any act in conflict with it void.

Thus he had it both ways. He avoided a losing confrontation with Jefferson, and he declared the Court's power to determine what was constitutional.

The case was, in reality, an exercise in political gamesmanship. Everyone agreed that in ordinary cases judges could read a law or a contract in dispute and say what it means.

THE COURT

But is the Constitution a law in this sense? Is it the charter of government, public guide, or a law as any other?

During his many years remaining on the Court, Marshall never used judicial review to overturn a Congressional law. By his acts, it's clear he believed it was a power to be used rarely and only in extraordinary cases in which a Congressional act was unarguably at odds with the Constitution. Otherwise, Congress deserved the benefit of the doubt. It was not the Court's place to meddle in policy, that is political, questions, Marshall said. Would that his successors believed the same.

CHAPTER SEVEN

Carol and I were slowly knitting together.

"You ever go over to the C & O Canal?" she asked.

"I bike it every once in a while," I said.

"I don't bike," she answered. "I tried it once and got a sore butt."

"It takes more than once," I said.

"Yeah, I'm sure," she said unconvincingly, "for a persistent type like you. You ever just walk it?"

I knew where she was going. "I would with the right invitation."

She laughed. For some reason our banter worked and she seemed to like it. "How about this Saturday morning?"

"Good," I said.

"Tell me how to find your place and I'll swing by and pick you up."

THE COURT

She was as good as her word. A little before nine I watched her come down my driveway, a long, single lane covered in crushed rock connecting my house to the Jimtown Road.

"It isn't hard to find," she said getting out of her car and coming up to the porch where I was sitting.

"No," I said.

"Nice view of Sugar Loaf," she said taking the rocker next to mine. "All this yours?" she asked, sweeping her arm in an arc over the front acres.

I nodded.

"But you don't farm it," she said.

"What makes you think I don't?" I asked flatly.

She gave me a look. "When? Between columns? Somehow I can't see you on a tractor."

"You caught me," I said. "Tom Evens farms it. I give him a cut price on the rent and he does all the yard maintenance and other outside work on the property, including keeping me supplied with fire wood. I have a small woods out back. He culls the dead fall every Autumn, keeps some and gives me the rest."

"Ooooh," she said. "You have a fireplace?"

"Big one," I said, "framed by stones taken from a nearby stream."

"Why from a stream?"

"The flowing water makes the stones nice and smooth. You can even see the fine grain in some of them, gray stippled with little white stripes."

She nodded as though it was obvious. "Going to invite me over some cold winter night to enjoy it? I'll bring the wine."

"Sounds like a plan," I said.

I was pleased and not totally surprised how easily it all flowed between us. I think we both saw something we wanted.

She drove to the Seneca aqueduct where there was a parking lot.

"Thought we'd walk west a couple of miles. Some nice river views and the Aqueduct is a nice sight."

It was, three graceful arches carrying the canal over Seneca Creek, the Potomac easily visible where the Seneca joined it. The aqueduct is made of Seneca red sandstone quarried nearby, an attractive stone also used to build the Smithsonian's Castle on the Mall.

I slung on my small backpack loaded with sandwiches, drinks and a couple of oranges. Carol planned a stop along the towpath where the river view was good. "I know just the spot," she said, "good for a picnic."

Carol did not waste a lot of time on small talk, something I liked, and didn't engage in business chat either.

We were just getting into our stride on the gritty surface of the tow path when she said, "I read your piece on Marbury. Political theater? Really? Every law school in the land will come down on you for that one." She laughed. Ironic?

"Colorful, I admit, but I'm trying to make a point with a nonlegal audience. Those law schools you have poised to drop on me like a load of law books want us to believe Marshall established a Constitutional right in that decision."

"Didn't he?"

"Did he?"

"Come on, I'm asking the questions, you're the witness."

"Yes, your honor."

"OK, stop it. So why didn't he establish judicial review?"

"Because it isn't his place to give the Court a power the Constitution hadn't given it. He said the Congress couldn't give him a power not mentioned in the Constitution. Why would he think he could do it for himself? He's using the specious argument that a written constitution sometimes needs to be interpreted just as any written document is.

"You have to assume all the members of the constitutional convention understood that. If they wanted the federal court system to have such an important power, why didn't they put it in? They were very explicit about what matters lay within the Supreme Court's original jurisdiction, matters between two or more states or questions regarding foreign officials on US soil. They left it to Congress to fill in the blanks for the rest of the federal court system, including the Supreme Court when it is acting as an appellate court. So, I repeat, if the Founding Fathers wanted the courts to have the power to overturn one of its laws, why didn't they say so?"

"Because it didn't need to? It's implied in the nature of courts, deciding disputes over the meaning of a law or a document?"

"That works if the meaning of a law or a contract is in dispute. A definitive answer binding on all is required. It's a standard function of most courts in civil or criminal cases. What the Constitution means is another matter."

"How so? When there is a dispute, who decides? Isn't the Constitution the supreme law of the land?"

"No. That's the kind of shit they say in law schools to make you think it's all so inevitable, descended from some Platonic realm of legal systems, immutable, accepted, beyond debate."

She laughed. "You're really on a roll."

"The Constitution is not a law, not in the usual sense of the word. It's a charter, not a law. It defines the institutions of government, creates their powers and defines who can be members of these institutions and under what conditions. It doesn't lay down ordinances requiring a certain behavior, like paying taxes, or forbidding others, such as discriminating on the basis of race, with penalties attached for violations."

"Mmmmm," she said. "But so do charters, no? What happens if Congress passes a law allegedly in violation of the Constitution? Let's say it breaks up California into three new states to create more senators, of interest to the majority party, but a clear violation of Article 4, section 3 of the Constitution? What does the judiciary do?" she asked.

"It does nothing unless California, whose agreement is constitutionally required, brings suit. If it doesn't, the assumption is it agrees. No suit, no decision. The Court is reactive, not proactive.

In all the cases I'm aware of, the Congress has exercised a power it clearly has. Several years ago a wealthy man running for the US Senate sued to overturn a law limiting the amount of his own money he could spend in supporting his candidacy. He claimed It was a violation of his

First Amendment rights. The Court agreed and overturned that part of the law.

"Article 1Section 4 clearly says Congress "...may at any time by Law make or alter such (electoral) regulations..." In other words, if Congress wants to regulate how much money an individual can spend in a federal election to keep the field level and free from the baneful affects of money, it has the Constitutional power to do so. Is Congress really limiting his speech by limiting the amount of his own money he can spend on his election?" The law applies to everybody and there is no penalty for opposing the law in speech, only for spending more than allowed.

"And that is not at the expense of his First Amendment rights?"

"Expense or just a condition of limitation."

"The First Amendment says Congress shall pass no law abridging the right of free speech."

"Yep, it does say that. Yet we limit speech in all sorts of ways. You can't walk into a Congressional session and harangue it to your heart's content, or tell a deliberate lie injurious to the social or material well-being of another. Imagine lying that a priest is a pederast. And you can't reveal government secrets. So we condition speech in all kinds of ways to protect the public good. What we don't do is criminalize speech when it's an expression of conscience, especially on public matters of wide common interest, as long as it doesn't lead to the immediate harm of others.

"So then what's so wrong with Congress limiting what he can spend of his own money to get elected to Congress? He isn't being penalized for opposing the law. He's free to do that as much as he likes. Congress isn't trying to shut him up. It's trying to control the corrosive effects of money in elections, keeping it fair for candidates of great means and not so great, prizing character and quality of ideas above money in our elections. If this crimps his exercise of speech in a mild way, so be it, a greater good is served, one more compelling than his ability to speak whenever, wherever and however he wants. The Court reasoned in a vacuum, where abstract rights live, not on the streets where the rest of us live, rubbing shoulders with other rights. It's legal theology, not democratic public policy. No right is absolute, including the right to life, and the limits we impose on them should be determined by the values of the society at large not by the dry, legal reasoning of insulated judges."

"Something to think about," she said.

We walked on, each lost in thought, until she exclaimed, "Ah, here we are."

'Here' was an open spot of the ground between the river and the tow path. Usually views of the river are obscured by a dense screen of trees. But this view was open of the river's quietly sparkling surface and ruffled patches of white water where it made another drop from its Appalachian sources. The opposite bank was a low cliff, the down river edge of the heights overlooking Harper's Ferry up river. We found a broad flat rock and sat.

"Sandwich?" I asked as I unzipped my rucksack.

"In a minute. I just want to sit and look first." She looked. Finally, she said, "Sometimes I just come out here to let this country wrap itself around me like a great cloak. It's comforting and defining, the way a good cloak is, makes an ordinary figure distinctive.

THE COURT

"Yeah, like that N.C. Wyeth illustration of Billy Bones in Treasure Island, Billy standing on a cliff top looking out to sea, his cloak blown out by the wind into something powerful and sinister."

She nodded. "It gives meaning, but I'm not thinking sinister. Far from it."

"No, you're thinking of this land and what it is, what make this part of Maryland different from all other places. It's not just a riverbank like any other, but the bank of the Potomac, one of nature's gems and a highway of our history. Here we're more than just an anonymous speck afloat in a featureless space, we're part of a definable, palpable presence. It's our home."

"Exactly," she said.

"I have similar feelings."

"You do?" she said, her voice up a level of excitement.

"Yeah. Why I moved here rather than somewhere on the Eastern Shore or the Shenandoa Valley. I've read a lot of Civil War history and I liked being in places with Civil War associations. The place is full of it. Lee crossed the Potomac at White's Ferry, just down river, to invade Maryland. I sometimes stand on the bank by the ferry and imagine his army wading across the river, the men holding their muskets aloft to keep them dry. Lee was looking for recruits, and to encourage Maryland to join the Confederate cause. So it's not just a pleasing country side, the country is also a river linking our present with our past. Same goes for Frederick. Market Street, there, and its side streets are a piece of a nineteenth century American red brick town. I feel that when I go there."

"You're a romantic," she said with a laugh.

"Look who's talking," I said.

"Yeah," she said, "I guess so. But I'd enjoy it more if it weren't for those weekend crowds on Market Street when I'm looking for a parking place."

"The price of success," I said.

"Yeah," she said, but why so steep?"

I could go on in my faux wise way, but I decided to just enjoy the moment, the sparkling river, the low palisade across the river, the canal at our backs, and her company.

Finally, she said, "You're quiet."

"Just enjoying it all," I said.

"Think I'll have that sandwich now," she said.

We ate and sipped our drinks.

A bald eagle swooped down the middle of the river. A brief splash and it rose from the water's surface and sped down river.

"Wow!" I exclaimed, "a bald eagle just snatched lunch."

"Where?"

"Out there, over the river, just to our left."

"Oh yeah. I can see the fish wriggling in its claws."

We watched as the eagle skimmed the river surface and then wheeled sharply up to the right to perch in the top branches of a tall tree.

"Just enjoying a little fish al fresco," I said.

She laughed. "Wouldn't see that just a few years ago."

"No, the river's better now, " I said, "the eagles are back doing what they've been doing since the river began. It's becoming a real river again."

THE COURT

She nodded. "We can even swim in the Potomac now. Did you know John Quincy Adams did that when he was president? Imagine a president doing that today."

"Yeah," I said, "but some things are still not better. Worse maybe."

"The Court?" she said.

"How'd you guess?" feigned surprise.

"I read your stuff. What else have you been talking about?"

We finished our lunch, sipped our drinks dry and took in one last time the lovely river scenes, ours free for the taking. We walked on for half hour up river and then turned to head back.

When we returned to my place she pulled up beside my car. There was a pause. Usually this is where you'd lean over for a kiss leading to who knows what.

"You going to show me that fireplace?" she said.

"Sure," I said. "Come on in."

It wasn't just the fireplace. Carol had something in mind. I let her set the pace, go where she wanted.

"You're right," she said "those stones are rustic. It fits"

I nodded. "A touch I added after moving in. I opened out the ground floor, too," sweeping my arms to take in the open space that had been separate living, dining room and kitchen, all open now in one flowing space dotted with furniture.

It's a nineteenth brick farmhouse, two stories, with a roofed galley running along one side of the second floor like a narrow porch. It's a feature peculiar to Maryland farmhouses of that era. It gives a good view of the sunsets over the blue line of mountains in the distance. Morning views are good, too, as the rising sun eats away the purple night shadows. My bedroom is just a few steps away.

    I walked through the house showing off its different features, Carol by my side coming closer and closer, almost like a young couple buying their first house. She didn't do things by accident. When we got to the upstairs porch, admiring the view of my field, soft and green under farmer Evan's alfalfa, with the Blue Ridge in Virginia marking the horizon, I leaned over and kissed her to say how glad I was she was there. She gave me a kiss back saying, 'let's get it on.'

CHAPTER EIGHT

It felt like home every time I entered the Standard's newsroom, its random chaos floating on a stream of purposeful activity, just what a good newsroom should be. That ambient noise masked a lot of creativity, the commotion just a release valve for the tensions caused by gathering facts and weaving them into a story someone'd like to read. I began my journalistic career there, and it was where our editor came out one day and said, "How'd you like to write a column?"

    I was there to attend a meeting of our executive editorial council, the think tank of the Standard's editorial pages, Jim McMahon, chief editor of the editorial pages, presiding. In addition to me there was Bob Suggs, Steve Archibald and Leroy Swann, all columnists cultivating different patches of the national political scene. Suggs had Congress, Archibald the executive, and Swan developments in the states that rose to national interest.

Just as an aside, Suggs is black. As a favor, Jim had not assigned him to cover racial matters. Bob repaid Jim's trust with good copy. All of Congress, and not just the Black Caucus, suited him just fine.

The Standard was engaged in a sustained effort to examine the deficiencies of our constitutional order, an 18th century document which we believed fell short of meeting the country's 21st century needs. Today's meeting was to see where we were and where we needed to go in the next several weeks..

"Great piece on the Court," Suggs said to me. "Marbury v Madison as political theater. Bet that gets a yowl from Yale and Harvard Law along with all the other Ivies."

"It's already started. I got a letter from Benjamin Shapiro, Professor of Constitutional Law at Yale."

"And he said what?" Archibald asked.

"In sum, my frivolous approach to one of the founding documents of our constitutional order showed how little I understood it."

"You expected anything different?" Steve asked.

"No, I guess it's par for the course, sadly. A little discussion rather than an ad hominem attack might have been better. I'd be interested to know why he thinks Marshall's personal opinion should have the same force as a provision of the Constitution.

"Worse, I got an unsigned letter from a concerned citizen who said I should be strung up to a light pole in front of the Standard as a warning to the unwise."

"I'd act surprised," Leroy Swann said, "except I'm not. There's too much of that shit going on. Trump's gone ten years now and this crap still happens?"

THE COURT

"Just the bleat of a defeated army in retreat," I said.

"Or the last bite of a dying snake," Jim McMahon said, "still dangerous."

"Right," Bob agreed, his pipe going full blast. "There are still small pockets of Trumpsters on the Hill, snakes, if you like."

"OK, none of this is getting us where we want to go today," Jim said. "Let's focus on what we want the next several weeks to look like."

"Carl," he said looking at me, "we need to keep the spotlight on the McDowell hearings. Let's hold his utterings on the Court up to the Constitution. So much of what he and those like him say come across as special judicial pleading, not solid Constitutional reasoning."

"I have some suggestions that might help," I said, "questions for the hearings. We might consider sending them to Senator Matthews for his take."

Senator Matthews, Jackson F Matthews of Wyoming, was chairman of the Senate Judiciary Committee. He saw eye to eye with us on the Court as well as the broader constitutional issues."

"Shoot," Jim McMahon said.

I cleared my throat, making Suggs laugh. We had a running gag about stuffy pretentious people. His Black humor worked like a heat seeking missile chasing a MIG.

"Okay, see what you guys think. First, Judge McDowell, how do you read Article 1, section 8, and Article lll, section 2 of the constitution? What are the implications of these for your position on the so-called separation of powers between Congress and the Court? Second, what is the Constitutional basis of judicial review? Third, why is it assumed judges are better qualified to sort out what are political rather than purely judicial issues? Is the Constitution a legal or a political document? If both, how do you distinguish them? Finally, what roles, if any in your opinion, do the Congress, the voters and the president play in deciding constitutional questions, or is this the exclusive preserve of the Court?

Suggs laughed. "Right on, the jugular."

"Good list as I see it" Jim said. "Anyone have anything to add?"

"Yeah, I do," Steve Archibald said. "Judge McDowell, if you were tasked with reforming the federal judiciary, including the Supreme Court, what reforms would you propose?"

"Good," I said, "I like it. Think he'd answer? It's a target on his back even before he's on the Court."

"If he's on the Court," Suggs said.

There was some more discussion on the Court and a few other items before Jim wrapped it up.

Senator Matthews office was in the Russell Senate Office Building, the oldest and in some respects the grandest of the several office buildings housing senators, representatives and their staffs. It was the first and, in some respects, the grandest of the four Congressional office buildings. Its stair banisters, for example, are of bronze while those of other House buildings are cast iron. The smaller Senate needs fewer offices leaving more money for frills. They're also a sign of the Senate's exalted opinion of itself.

The Senator's office was on the second floor. The entry way to his suite is dominated by a spot lit western saddle

THE COURT

of finely tooled leather, reminding visitors that Wyoming's senior senators once spent long days in the saddle ranging over his large cattle ranch.

He was waiting for me behind his large desk, behind him the gleaming white dome of the Capitol nicely framed in a large window.

I gave the picture an admiring gaze.

"Reminds me of why I'm here," he said, noticing my gaze. He held out his hand. "Always good to see you, Carl."

"Likewise, Senator,"

"Jim McMahon said we should talk. The McDowell hearing are two weeks off and we need to make sure we're all riding the same trail," he said, his fondness for down home range talk well known. "Some questions, Jim said?"

"That's right, Senator," I said drawing them from my brief case and handing them to him. He was in his mid-sixties but still looked fit and trim enough for a day in the saddle, the fringe of white hair circling his bald pate notwithstanding.

His eye ran quickly over the list of questions. Then he looked up at me. "Looks like our minds are two streams running in the same direction. Have some of the same questions in mind myself. I like the one about reforming the court."

"Think he'd answer? Won't he dodge, calling the question hypothetical?"

"He might. Won't work. Too much deference for the Court in the past, like it was a church. Protected them then, not now. New times. We're tired of the dodge followed by something different once they're on the Court. We used to buy the package because the wrapping was pretty. Now we want to know what's in the box. He wants our vote, he answers our questions. The Federalist Society doesn't put up with such cute silence. They damn well want to know what you think before they sign on, and now we do too. No answer, no support."

Back in my farmhouse I sat down to write. McDowell, unlike almost all his predecessors, chose the opposite of silence on the public podium. He sees himself as the judicial gunslinger defending the virgin Court against the hot breathed politicians. "The Congress," he now writes in an oped piece in the New York times, "has no right to legislate a code of ethics for the Supreme Court. This," he proclaims," violates the sacred separation of powers laid down by our Founding Fathers."

I wrote, "What Constitution is he reading and what separation is he taking about? Article l, section 8 among all the other powers granted Congress is the power to "…constitute Tribunals inferior to the supreme Court."

'Aha' he will respond, 'you are overlooking the word 'inferior.'

"No, dear judge, I am not. The Court in its original jurisdiction is established by the Constitution, a jurisdiction narrowly confined to matters arising between two or more states or involving foreign officials on US soil. In all other respects it is the last link in the judicial appellate system, and that is created by Congress. Just read Article lll, section 2, paragraph 2. The '…Court when not exercising original jurisdiction… shall have appellate jurisdiction…with such Exceptions, and under such regulations as the Congress shall make.'

THE COURT

"In other words, dear Judge, when you justices of the Court are hearing a case on appeal, by far the most numerous and juiciest part of your work, Congress has a say in your business, not to control your search for justice, but to affect the conditions under which you conduct that search. That includes ethical rules. It also sets the number of justices, their salary and funds the courthouse. In return Congress has a right to set conditions for accepting your appointment, your salary along with all the other conditions."

I sat back and read it over and then went out for a bike ride, content with a good day's work.

CHAPTER NINE

"You like Italian food?" Carol and I no longer went to Patty's Patio to meet. We just called. My cell phone began its melodious shaking as soon as I walked in from my bike ride. Carol knows the good buttons to push.

"Is the pope Catholic?" I asked, a lousy imitation of Italian sarcastic. "You know I spent four years in Rome as bureau chief."

"I do," she said, patiently as with a loved but sometimes difficult child. "So I'm cooking Italian tonight. Come over about six," she paused for effect, "and bring your toothbrush."

Italian turned out to be not just cooking in the Italian way but presenting in the Italian way as well. First came the ante pasta, roasted zucchinis, peppers and artichokes, then the pasta dish, sized Italian, half the size of the large mound of pasta Americans get, followed by meat, potatoes and veggies. Dolce-desert-comes last.

THE COURT

I had to look twice at the pasta dish. Not red like most pasta sauces, brownish. I didn't say anything. One thing with Carol, assume she knows what she's doing. She usually does.

"What the...? I said with the first bite. She was watching, a barely suppressed smile.

"Truffles!" I exclaimed. "How in the hell do you...?"

"Know how to make truffle sauce?"

"Uh Uh," I said thru a mouthful. Truffle sauce like this in America? One of my fondest Italian memories is of this black truffle sauce made by a restaurant in Umbria I went to frequently. It had a great view of Spoleto and its black truffle sauce was to die for. It was not a sauce from the Betty Crocker Cookbook."

"I didn't know that" she said. "Good guess."

"How did you learn to make it? Don't tell me its an old recipe from your mother. Who in America knows about black truffles. You've not been to Italy, right?"

"Right, I haven't," her teasing smile still in place.

"So how?" I took another bite. Yep, it was real truffle sauce.

"I once did some legal work for an Italian woman from their embassy. She was a lawyer. We became friends. She wanted to know more about the American legal system, I wanted to learn some Italian dishes. I gave her legal pointers, and she taught me some Italian recipes. This is one of them."

"She from Umbria by any chance?"

"Why Umbria? Says she grew up in a town named Todi. She lives in Rome now."

"Brown Todi, resplendent in a soft wash of sunlight on its hill," I said.

"What?"

"Line I wrote in a piece about Umbria years ago," I said. "I called it the soul of Italy. St. Francis, and all that good cooking. Todi is a prominent Umbrian town with a mediaeval past."

"But what made you think of Umbria?"

I told her about the restaurant and its sauce "I went there often.
The food is superb. After my first meal I always had cognac. About my seventh time there the owner brought out every bottle of cognac he had on a tray, laid it on the table and said, "Prego."

"What's prego mean?"

"Please, meaning I was free to whichever I wanted and as much as I wanted.

'Good public relations," she said.

"The human touch," I said, "never far away when dealing with Italians."

"Even the Mafia?"

"They're bastards, but human bastards, not ideological bastards like the Nazis."

"Interesting distinction. Not sure the law would see the difference."

She was just musing harmlessly, not launching in a new direction.

Instead she brought out the meat dish, a scallopine d' lemoné, delicate, subtle and balanced like the best of Italian cuisine.

THE COURT

"That Italian friend of yours knew what she was doing," I said. "This is really good. Keep feeding me like this and..."

She nodded at the compliment. "Prego," she said with a laugh. "I know some other dishes, too. We'll try them another time."

The meat dish was followed by a gelato that she must have gone to Frederick for. "I don't have any cognac," she said, "but I do have something very Italian."

"Grappa," I exclaimed.

"Knew you'd guess it."

Not just Grappa, but Grappa in the kind of glasses Italians drink their Grappa, tall, tapered, thick and narrow at the bottom, wide at the top. Grappa is the Italian Schnapps, wine distilled into a clear, potent drink, a first cousin of cognac. No Italian meal is complete without it, so I like to think.

We moved to her couch covered in a bright flora pattern. She had spent some money fixing up her country digs.

"I have a question," she said after we had sipped our way through our Grappas and I was started on a second.

"Yeah?" I said.

"Your piece about Marbury v Madison. Marshall moves the case from the district court to the Supreme Court to evade the Judiciary Act of 1789 which gives federal courts the power to issue writs of mandamus. Why was he so certain the Judiciary Act couldn't apply to the Supreme Court in its original jurisdiction?"

"Maybe he wasn't, but he wasn't interested in clarifying the point. He wanted to make a pronouncement bolstering the legitimacy of the Court. The Congress, he said, could not add a power to his original jurisdiction not there by the Constitution. That was the point he was trying to make, he says what the Constitution means. The point is arguable, it seems to me. The Congress can't expand the Court's original jurisdiction, but why couldn't it empower the Court to issue writs of mandamus when exercising its original jurisdiction? It's a standard part of any court's kit and it would make the exercise of original jurisdiction far more effective. It's an open question as far as I'm concerned, strict construction v non strict construction, neither one necessarily offensive to the Constitution."

"Fair point," she said. "After all, the Congress has a lot to say on the construction of the Supreme Court in both its original and appellate jurisdictions. It says how many judges there will be to hear cases under either jurisdiction, how often, what they're paid, where they will be housed and so forth. If Congress can say there shall be five, or nine or twelve judges on the Court, why can't it also say the Supreme Court in its original jurisdiction can issue writs of mandamus? You're right, strict or loose, both could work constitutionally. You sure you didn't go to law school?"

The Grappa was spreading like slow fire through my veins. I kept looking at how her green eyes changed shade with each changing mood as she talked at how leonine her mane of tawny hair was, not lawyer-lady like at all, and the way she could put together such a wonderful meal. In a burst of enthusiasm, I blurted out "What a gift you are."

She smiled and said,"Well, if I'm a gift, why don't you unwrap me?"

CHAPTER TEN

Every once in a while I put the bike on the car and drive over to the Antietam battlefield to ride its paved paths and the winding country roads surrounding it. It's perfect biking. Hills in the distance, some of which figured in the battle, add a blue border to the terrain.

The two armies were separated by Antietam Creek, Lee's on the west bank and McClellan's Union forces on the east side of the broad stream. It was an important feature of the battle, a moat for Lee, an obstacle for McClellan.

There was one spot that could be crossed unopposed, out beyond Lee's left flank. McClellan sent a large force there to launch an early morning attack on Lee's left flank, held by Jackson's Corps, of Stonewall fame. To tangle with Stonewall was to know what war was all about.

While this attack was progressing, McClellan planned to feint towards Lee's center guarding the bridge into the town of Sharpsburg and attack Lee's right flank across another bridge farther downstream, both actions to keep Lee busy while his left flank was being rolled up.

It was a good plan and might have worked if all the Union commanders moved all at once and kept a steady pressure on Lee, inferior in numbers to them.

If they understood, they didn't execute. They attacked seriatim rather than in one thunderous blow. Their piecemeal assault allowed Lee to switch forces back and forth between hot sports. Union forces suffered accordingly.

Even so, after some bloody switching back and forth by Lee, McClellan's men did manage to bend Lee's left back while troops under General Burnside crossed the Antietam under fire to threaten Lee's right wing and center. At day's end the Union army stood ready to decisively close with Lee on the morrow and break his bleeding line, helped by a fresh corps that had yet to enter the fight. Coming on top of the battle's already large butcher's bill, this blow could be mortal to Lee's battered forces. Seeing this, and with the Potomac at his back, an obstacle against which he could be bashed, Lee withdrew under cover of darkness.

McClellan preened and claimed a glorious victory.

Victory, yes, glorious maybe not. Why, Lincoln asked with poorly hidden exasperation, had McClellan not driven Lee into the Potomac and destroyed him. It could have ended the war or, at least, hastened its end.

Still, incomplete though it was, the victory gave Lincoln the opportunity he needed to issue his Emancipation Proclamation. That changed the war from a war against rebellion to a war against slavery. It also reduced almost to zero recognition of the Confederacy by the major European powers who could not ally themselves with slavery happy though they might have been to see the American colossus cut down a peg.

It wasn't such large thoughts as these that occupied me as I took a breather by the Corn Field, the long, broad field of shoulder high corn where the battle was first joined early on that morning. Union force attacking down the Hagerstown Pike collided with part of Jackson's forces hidden in the Corn Field's tall stalks. As the Union forces approached, the Confederates stood up and opened a withering fire. The Union forces replied in kind, and the fight was on. For more than two hours the fight swayed back and forth ghoulishly lit by lightening sheets of musketry and long tongues of cannon fire until the Confederates were forced grudgingly back to new positions.

What made this battle bloody, as it had so many others early in the war, was the killing power of the Civil War musket. It was much greater than its predecessors. The lethal reach of those older muskets was around a hundred yards; the lethal reach of these, carried by both Union and Confederate infantry, was closer to five hundred yards. Yet the tactics both sides used in attack were of massed lines moving upright in close order on the enemy, the tactics of the earlier muskets.

It was said after the engagement no stalk of corn remained upright in the Corn Field, and those walking from one side of the field to the other could not do so without stepping on corpses. Perhaps both statements are exaggerations, but if so, not by much, given the casualties rendered that day by one of the bloodiest days ever fought by US troops.

What I was thinking as I looked over that large field, swaying with shoulder high corn as it was on that smoke filled day, was of the raw courage that enabled the infantrymen on both sides, blue and gray, to go toe to toe for several terror filled hours, launching one deadly fusillade after another. It was not child's play.

I thought, too, of the hand the Supreme Court bore in bringing the nation to this pass.

In 1858 Dred Scott, a slave in Missouri, sued for his freedom. He had been taken in his earlier life to the Northwest Territory where slavery was banned by Congress. That made him a free man, he contended, citing the the Northwest Ordinance and the Constitution's Article IV, Section 3. The Ordinance forbade slavery in the territory before any part of it became a state. The power of Congress to do this came from Article 3 which says "... Congress shall have the power to... make all needful Rules and Regulations respecting the Territory... belonging to the United States..."

The Court could have simply answered Scott's question: yes, or no. Instead, inspired by Chief Justice Taney, it moved the case to a broader judicial field to answer two questions: what federal rights do blacks, slave or free, have, and does Congress have the power to bar slavery in US lands not yet states? The South was looking for a particular answer.

To Scott the Court said, you have no rights the federal Constitution is bound to respect, so take you suit and go home. To Congress it said, you cannot deprive a slave owner of his property without due process, a right guaranteed by the 5th Amendment. Article IV of the Constitution and the Northwest Ordinance both are trumped by the Bill of

Rights. The Missouri Compromise is also overturned for the same reason.

The Constitution was at war with itself, and the Court, using due process, was the peace maker.

This was the first time the Court declared a Congressional act unconstitutional.

Dred Scott fanned the already roaring flames of the slavery issue by taking it out of the political realm and plunking it down in the judicial. That drove the nation closer to war.

The negotiation and compromise of politics, the kind that fashioned the Missouri Compromise, was just what settling the status of the new Kansas and Nebraska territories required. Unfortunately this kind of politics was subverted by Dred Scott which set the slavery issue in judicial concrete allowing slavery to go wherever the South wished it to go. Congress was powerless to stop it.

But even without Dred Scot, politics might not have been able to bridge the yawning gap between a South of prideful, arrogant, narrow minded slave owners and a North of morally troubled citizens slowly realizing a nation could not endure half slave and half free. Bridging the gap was the nation's great task, and it was a job well beyond the Court.

I looked over the Corn Field, in my imagination smelling the battle smoke and hearing the desperate sounds of that hot September day, a deadly cacophony in part the fruit of Dred Scott which had left the South feeling entitled and the North feeling betrayed. When Lincoln, who opposed the extension of slavery into the territories not yet states, was elected the South felt violated and the North felt vindicated.

WILL SUTTER

War came.
The Court had served the nation badly.
I put these thought into my next column.

CHAPTER ELEVEN

As the McDowell hearings drew closer the Standard's campaign for Constitutional change intensified. Our strategy meetings increased to twice weekly.

"Set in judicial concrete. That was good," Leroy Swann said. "It's about time someone said these things out loud. The Court has gotten away with way too much because of an exaggerated respect for it. The line between it as a court of law and it as an political policy making body grows less and less distinct each year. I guess, along with everyone else, I was just going along with the flow until your columns. Good work."

"Thanks," I said, and meaning it. I respected Leroy's opinion. "And I like your pieces on rank order voting. Sounds like a plan for congressional elections. From what you've said it would increase popular support and eliminate Gerrymandering. That's a lot right there."

Leroy had written a series of articles on states that were adopting the rank order system and multi member congressional districts, making it easier for more than two candidates to run, widening the avenue for third party candidates and making it more likely that the candidates with the widest support are elected. It also makes it more difficult for extreme candidates to win. Most voters lean toward the middle. Some argue it will take longer to count the votes and rank order may be confusing to voters, though the evidence for this is weak.

"Remind me again, Leroy, how it all works."

"Fairly simple," he said.

"It isn't as effective in district where only two candidates are contending for one office though even there it does have its uses. The two candidates are in effect rank ordered; a vote for one is not a vote for the other. it works best when many candidates are running for the same office or if a number of candidates are running in a multi member district. "

"Okay," I doubtfully said, playing the uniformed reader.

"Let's go through the different scenarios."

There was something of the teacher in Leroy.

"First one, a single member district, like most Congressional districts. Usually only two candidates run. But now, under rank ordering, we have four people running. Before such a number often meant no one got a majority and a runoff had to be held. But under rank order it's different. Voters now rank order the four candidates, marking their choice as number, one, two, three and four. Let's say the candidates are Smith, Jones, Brown and Greene. None of them gets fifty one percent of the vote so we go to round two."

THE COURT

"A runoff, you mean?"

"Nope," he said. "Not under rank order voting."

"How so?" I asked. I thought I knew, but wanted to make sure.

"Okay, we have these four candidates none of whom got a majority. Now, instead of a runoff the candidates are ranked according to their vote totals as first, second choice and so forth. The candidate with the lowest total is eliminated."

"So all the votes for them are wasted?"

"Not entirely. All those who made this candidate their first choice have their second-choice vote added to the totals of their second choice candidate. Let's say voter one made Greene their first choice and Jones their second choice. Greene is eliminated because of he is lowest ranking and Jones receives one more vote.

"At the end of the count candidates are once more ranked and the lowest ranked is again eliminated with all the second-choice ballots assigned as before. Again no one has a majority (if ones does, they win) so we go to round two. Again the candidate with the lowest total is eliminated and all the second choice ballots are added to the totals of the appropriate candidates.

"Now a third count is made of the totals of the two remaining candidates and the candidate with the highest total of first and second choice ballots wins.

"The beauty of this system is that the candidate who won the most first and second choice ballots will likely be the candidate most of the voters wanted. It allows more people into the race, encourages more variety and usually results in the more moderate candidates winning.

"Let's say among the four candidates one preferred universal health care, one favored government backed care only for those with incomes below a certain level, one favored it just for seniors and one favored private insurance over public plans. In a two-person race in a swing district shading slightly conservative the candidate favoring private insurance might squeak through, his conservative stand on other issues giving him a slight edge. Yet, close to a majority of voters favored one or another of the competing positions on health care and almost all made their second-choice candidates one who favored one or another of the public health care versions.

Quite possibly enough of these second-choice votes would have given one of these three candidates a majority over the candidate favoring no public health care insurance. In short, those who wanted some form of public support for health care insurance would win over the candidate who wanted none, even though he might have won in a head-to-head race. In a head-to-head race slightly less than half the voters would have been completely disappointed on the health care issue, under rank order voting they had a better chance of at least some satisfaction.

The Standard was addressing a wide sweep of political issues on the assumption the Constitution, an 18th century document, could no longer adequately address the needs of a 21st century country. The Electoral College, the skewed representation of the Senate, the variety of electoral practices for federal office found in the states, the role of money in elections and in our legislative politics, and a court system that presumed to hold a superior power of judgement over the other two branches of government, despite no Constitutional power to do so, all cried out for close examination. There were even mutterings that we would be better off with a parliamentary system of government.

Steve Archibald proposed it and Jim Martin was clearly falling in with him. I suspected Suggs was as well.

I was a little hesitant about this one myself. "Why," I asked the group, when the idea was first broached, "a parliamentary system?"

"It concentrates responsibility, for one thing," Jim Main answered.

I was a little surprised that Jim, who was usually so cautious in his advocacy, came out so flat footedly in support of what was certainly a radical proposal.

"How so?" I asked, catching at least some of his drift and thus suspecting already the answer.

"Right now responsibility is divided between the president and the congress. Let's say a presidential candidate runs on universal health care. Some running for the Senate and the House support this, but several others don't, some wanting it only for seniors, others only for lower income people. The president in favor of universal health care wins, but the Congress is a patch work with support split among one or another of the diluted versions of health care, some others favor only private insurance, no government involvement. So what is the government's policy on health care? Is it universal health care as advocated by the president or some watered down version of it from Congress? Who is to be held responsible for success or failure in resolving the health care issue? The President? The Congress? Who? If that can't be decided, then is anyone responsible?"

"OK, I get that," I said. "But how does a parliamentary system make matters better?"

"By making the parliament and only the parliament fully responsible for the actions of the government. There is no split responsibility."

"They can't hold the executive branch responsible without endangering the parliament?"

"No. The parliament appoints the members of the executive branch, including the leader or prime minister, usually members of the governing party or coalition in parliament. They follow the directions of the parliament. If they don't, and this includes the prime minister, parliament can remove them. There is no claim of executive privilege and there is no division of powers as in our system.

"In an election each party goes before the electorate with its program… If they win and don't implement the promised program, they will have to answer for it at the next election. Political responsibility is concentrated in one place, there is no finger pointing as with us because there is no one to point fingers at; it is us."

The more Jim talked the more I liked what I was hearing. It was clear the Standard was in for the long haul.

CHAPTER TWELVE

By now Carol and I were falling into certain comfortable routines. We'd be known as a couple even if we didn't look at ourselves that way. We weren't a couple according to some definition or plan of relationships espoused by some journal of good living; we were growing organically. We both had at that point in our lives room for a serious someone else. We were both divorced, we both had grown children with full lives of their own, who were not yet an integral part of what was happening between us, we both were well established in our careers, probably past the mid-point for each of us, and we just liked being together, domestically, socially, intellectually and sexually. It was the full load.

We were both enough of an age not to be entranced by all the glitz accompanying male female relationships so fascinating to younger folks. Maybe that's nature's way of saying to the youngsters, get on with it, nature awaits. But we had gotten on with it and were still within easy reach of those natural urges that set one aflame. Our sexual life was happy and exuberant. We both had been around long enough to understand in addition to the fire and passion of younger sex, there was also an intimacy and depth that left us smiling.

I was pleased to discover a capacity for tenderness I may not have thought much about before. Now I took delight in the sweet exploration of those moments of physical intimacy when there was nothing between us but what nature gave us at birth. I fell into such stroking and speaking that fit no other moment but that. Once, when we went from a soft pink to a bright red she said when we had finished, "when you do that thing you do I feel like a flower opening up to the sun."

That said it all for me.

The intellectual part was as important to both of us. Her concentration was the law and mine public affairs, but there was plenty of overlap. We had lots to talk about. Law was her focus, largely on behalf of public officials caught up, usually as innocent victims, in some partisan food fight. Lawyers, as everyone knows, cost money.

"Phil Hines was in that position," she explained one day as we were talking about some of the down sides of our professions. "He was assistant secretary of defense for procurement accused of corruption by a Senator. There was no formal indictment, but Phil was subpoenaed to appear before the Senate Committee for Defense to answer the Senator's accusation."

"Was there actual corruption?"

"Certainly not in the legal sense though a certain legal exposure remained, remote, but enough to make legal counsel at the hearings advisable. He was steered to us because we were good at that kind of representation. We're not cheap."

"And I suspect he was not rich, making his legal fees a serious financial burden, one he would not be facing if he were not a civil servant?

"You got it."

"What was the senator's beef?"

"Defense had not purchased a big-ticket item from a contractor in his state. He accused the Pentagon, namely my client, of taking bribes. At the hearing, Phil was subjected to a vitriolic stream of suggestive statements and innuendoes the purpose of which was not to uncover wrongdoing on Phil's part but to pressure the Pentagon to use his contractor the next time. To protect himself Phil had to retain us. It was unfair, and I wish I could have represented him pro bono, but the firm wouldn't hear of it. Pro bono for him could mean pro bono for every government official in Phil's predicament. It's a lucrative field for us. But it's so unfair."

My fraught spot was protecting confidential sources for a hot story. The trick was to write the story with full justice while not exposing the vulnerable source. Sometimes it was almost impossible and my choice was kill the story or put my source at serious risk.

"So what did you do? She asked.

"Give them the choice. A person's life is more important than the public's right to know the full dimensions of some scandal. I would do all I could to find another source. If not, kill the story. Bottom line, thwarting some pocket lining boondoggle or act of political selfishness was not worth destroying the life of some innocent party.

I thought for a minute. "This all reminds me of an idea I had some time ago in a similar situation. A colleague at the Standard who was protecting a source was indicted for obstruction of justice. Had the paper not made the case its own, she would have had to deal with the legal expenses herself."

"You talking about the Wrigley case?"

"Yeah, you know it?"

"Of course. It was in the news. A source in the State Department I recall."

"Yeah, that's right."

"So the standard did fund her defense?"

"It did and rightly so. The government was just harassing her because it wanted to know who the whistle blower was. It alleged exposure of classified information, but that was bogus. No classified information was involved. It was a case of CYA, cover your ass, by some high-ranking State official whom Margaret's story would make look stupid. We were a little surprised the administration took matters so far, but it had been dinged several times by unflattering stories fed by internal leaks. They used this case as a shot across the bows of the media and possible leakers. The suit was meant to keep the government from looking bad, not protect classified information. The Standard, to its credit, did not hang Margaret out to dry and force her face either expensive legal bills or possible jail time."

"I remember the case" Carol said. The issue was, as I recall, publishing in good faith information the media had no real way of knowing was classified information. The assurance was it was confidential information but not secret. In fact, some of it was top secret, but she didn't know that.

So is she guilty of revealing government secrets when she didn't know it was secret?"

"Yeah, that's right. Margaret was being used as a test case."

"The staked goat to lure out the leaker or at least discourage them?"

"Something like that, though I don't think Margaret would appreciate being characterized as a goat. She sees herself more as a journalistic tiger, sorry, tigress, apologizes to Margaret."

Carol laughed. "I like her already. But my point is, Margaret was being used as a way to discourage leakers, collateral damage."

I laughed. "I'm sure she'd be happier with that, sounds more persecuted, victim like.

"But how did that generate your idea?"

"Margaret got tangled up in what could have been a potentially expensive legal fight not through any fault of hers. She was doing her job as a journalist, keeping the public informed. A lot of people in public life get entangled needlessly in expensive legal embroilments, especially members of the press or ranking government official caught up in partisan skirmishing with possible criminal indictment staring them in the face. It's true for private citizens as well who are wrongly accused of a felony and forced to go into debt to keep out of jail."

"I was about to say life is unfair, but I know that's no answer. So where are you going with this?"

Carol was a good listener. She had strong opinions of her own, but she would hear you out.

"I liken the jeopardy to legal danger to the jeopardy our health faces from disease and accident. Medical expenses are often beyond average means. Society's answer is medical insurance."

"OK, now I see where you're going. Legal insurance?"

"Right, insurance to cover your legal liabilities the way medical insurance covers medical expenses."

"This would be voluntary, like life insurance?"

"No, mandatory, as I think health care insurance ought to be."

"Wow, that's a big bite! And how exactly would this work?"

"It would be paid for by a modest tax on every taxpayer. Every lawyer would be enrolled in a College of Attorneys the way all British doctors are enrolled in their National Health Service."

"You mean required to provide legal services to defendants? Free of charge?"

"Not exactly. Your tax is your fee. Would work just like Medicare."

"And you get to choose your lawyer?"

"No. One is assigned to you. You are charged with murder, a lawyer with that criminal experience would be assigned as your defense.'

"What if you get a shitty lawyer. A lot's at stake."

"All members of the College have to be professionally qualified to a high and rigorous standard and adequately supported."

"Fine. But why not allow choice of attorney?"

"I'd be willing to consider it. However, one objective of the program is to ensure that your defense is not highly determined by your bank account or lack of it, as is true currently. A poor Black from the 'hood accused of murder has to settle for a court appointed attorney for his defense, while a famous Black athlete can afford the dream team. If the quality of justice drops as the gentle rain, shouldn't it drop equally on all, rich and poor?"

'OK, I get the general principle, but maybe allowing the defendant some choice in attorney wouldn't compromise that? Might make the proposal more acceptable."

"A fair point."

"Another question."

"Shoot."

"Would this apply just to criminal cases but not civil?"

"I'd have to think about that. My focus is on criminal matters with jail time involved. But I would include civil cases such as the two we discussed earlier."

"You're way ahead of your time. Can you imagine how the lawyers will react to this, especially criminal lawyers who make big bucks defending rich crooks?"

"I'm not naive. Of course they will resist, just as the AMA resisted universal health care when Truman proposed it, though now they favor it. Lawyers might see things differently, too, after some thought. In any case, our leaders should lead as well as listen. Naturally the doctors and lawyers would resist corporatization of their professions, as least the Lone Rangers will, who rake it in. Yes, the wealth of some will be less but the gains to the public good would be greater. Is the essence of a community to protect the right of an enterprising few to make as much moolah as possible, regardless of consequences to the rest, or is it to insure as high a floor of prosperity and security as possible for the many?

"I get your argument, but it would be a tough slog politically. Money talks with us. Those who have it want to keep it."

"Serious campaign reform making elections at public expense would seriously mute the voice of money. That would help."

"An idealist, too, I see," she said with a gentle laugh.

"No, a realist. Most European liberal democracies control the use of money in elections, so why can't we? In fact we did at one time. McCain Feingold? The Supreme Court took care of that by declaring McCain Feingold unconstitutional. You're right, money talks, and not just in elections. The Court, too."

We spent many an evening like this, and then relaxed by streaming something good. I liked a lot of the European offerings, more substance, less glitz.

Then we might sing a sweet song in bed. Passion and tenderness weren't just for the young.

There are times I'm so happy I invited myself to sit that morning at Patty's Patio.

CHAPTER THIRTEEN

The war over McDowell nomination was shifting into high gear. He was on his soap box again, defying the Senate's efforts to throw a halter over the Supreme Court's horse.

"This," he proclaimed, "would violate the sacred principle of separation of powers and attempt to hobble the institution most dedicated to protecting the rights of citizens against an overweening congress and executive. The Court must remain free and unfettered."

Nothing like arming up to protect the innocent," I thought. I went to my computer and dug in.

"Yes, protector of the Rights of Man. Without the Court, the average citizen would be naked before the self-serving aggressions of a tyrannical government, says McDowell. What does history say?

"One recalls the way the Court stood up to the Federalists in the 1790s when they passed the Sedition Act making criminal those who defamed, brought into contempt, inspired hatred of, or stirred up sedition against

Congress or the President. Constructive criticism of the government was permitted, as long as it was polite, not defamatory or insulting. Problem was, many editors, especially those who supported Jefferson, routinely dipped their quills in vitriol. They were jailed. You could respectfully question President Adams' Quasi War against the French, but if in your righteous ardor you wrote 'that tub of lard in the White House is endangering the country," you faced indictment. The advice from the protector of the common man who upheld the law? 'Watch your mouth.'

"Decades later the Court struck another blow for the common man this time in the person of Dred Scot, the slave who sued for his freedom. His master had brought him to the Northwest territory years earlier where slavery was banned by the Northwest Ordinance. Forget it, this defender of the underprivileged said, a black man, slave or not, has no rights the constitution is bound to respect. That included the citizenship enjoyed by some blacks in northern states.

"The Court continued after the Civil War to defend the big interests against the average citizen. When some mid-western states tried to stop predatory railroads from shearing their farmers like so many sheep, the Court batted them down. Railroads, the Court asserted, were private property, and private property was protected by the Constitution's due process. Profits as much as engines, box cars or rails, were property and could not be seized by mere legislation. By the law of divine economics, the vulnerable must stand naked before the powerful.

"The result? Powerful railroads were free to take as much as they liked from the pockets of individual farmers for carrying their grain to market. That's how the Constitutionally enshrined Free Market worked, the judges said. Farmers were, of course, free to find other means of getting their grain to market just as they had before the railroads. The government had no place in the process.

The Court's expansive reading of the Fifth Amendment and its focused application to such economic questions undercuts the give and take of politics which is more responsive to the many currents moving the public's thinking. The Court's legalistic reasoning might work well in a court room, it was disastrous in the fields and streets where most of the public lived. It did little to settle questions of fairness and communal harmony, though big money had no complaints. Which serves the public better, dry "Constitutional" reasoning, or democratically responsive politics?

"Too often the Court uses one part of the Constitution, the First Amendment or the due process clauses of the 5th and 14th Amendments to undermine the powers of Article I. The due process of the Fifth Amendment was meant to prevent the government from arbitrarily seizing homes, papers and goods the way British authorities had done to obstreperous colonists, and the Fourteenth Amendment's was there to protect the civil rights of recently freed slaves in the former Confederate states. To use them to protect big money is a perversion.

"And what exactly is due process? Just the proceedings of a court, or any regular generally agreed upon procedures of the government, including legislation?

"Taxes and any form of economic regulation-the entire commerce clause-would be near impossible with such a reading. Any time the Court pleased it could stop a tax or halt a regulation, turning the powers of Congress into hostages of the Court's latest Constitutional theory. This is government by unelected court rather than an elected Congress.

"Who is better at unraveling the knotty political, economic and social issues bedeviling any society? The Court with its abstract, specialized, dry legal procedures, or the legislatures, firmly rooted in the society, elected as they are by the people, and ultimately responsible to them? The Constitution says, Congress. Got a complaint? Vote the bums out. Try that with the Court.

"We have a written constitution whose provisions are not up for debate or pragmatic haggling; I'm sure Mr. McDowell will say.

"Well, yes and no. We have a written Constitution whose terms are drawn very broadly. It is not a detailed contract with clearly written terms whose powers and limits are clearly and exhaustively defined.

"Wrong, Mr. McDowell would argue. What is not included cannot be claimed, and what is included is not subject to multiple or arbitrary interpretations. There is one meaning and one only, and that is best discernable by the Court. The Constitution is the Bible of our democracy, the Court, its Temple, and the justices its high priests. What they saith goes.

"Really? A Bible? The Constitution says what, but not how. It confers the power to tax and regulate commerce but not a word on how that is to be done. Who best to check Congressional use of these powers, voters or judges?

"The Court says it is because it is impartial. The Constitution is a contract and conformity to its terms best judged by a Court. The Standard says, as the country said during much of the nineteenth century, We the People, the voters, are. The Preamble begins We the People, and We can read the Constitution as easily as the judges can.

"We will have more to say on this topic in subsequent columns."

"You guys are not holding back," Carol said with a dry laugh.

We were walking the canal tow path, by now almost a Saturday routine. Great Falls was our destination.

"You were right when you said we are in full combat mode. The Standard is determined to rein in the Court."

"Just one of your goals, if I'm reading right," she said. "I've been reading the columns of Suggs and Archibald. Sounds almost like a revolution to me."

"We're aiming high" I replied. "Our political apparatus is creaking; it's not working as it needs to. We are alone among the developed nations without universal health care. High medical bills not covered by insurance can still bankrupt us. That doesn't happen in England, or Germany or any of the other liberal democracies. US elections are heavily affected by money, special interests too often drowning out character and quality of ideas. That's much less true in the other democracies. These are just two areas crying out for reform. It's part the work of special interests and part the fracturing of power among several institutions making manipulation easier. In a parliamentary system it is centered in the elected parliament."

"Yet that is what the Founding Fathers wanted."

"It is and it may have met their needs then but it doesn't meet our needs now, not completely. They had just emerged from a history in which Britain arbitrarily governed the colonies with minimum consultation, especially on important matters like taxation. The colonies had little real voice in matters that directly affected them. The Founders wrote a constitution that was in part a reaction to what they saw as a dangerous concentration of power between the Crown and the Parliament, devising a government that resembled a car with the steering wheel on one side and the brake pedals and accelerator on the other, accident free but of poor mobility."

Carol laughed. "So you're willing to risk more accidents just so you can get were you want to go, safety features or no?

"We want a government going where the people want it to go without a high risk of serious accidents. Its chief safety feature is elections. As long as we can change a government that is speeding or driving recklessly, we have effectiveness and safety.

"And the Court," I asked her, "any reforms you think?" She made her living writing briefs to be argued before the Court.

She shrugged. "I get some of your points. The Court is way out of its lane and needs correction, if not reform. It has to back off its presumed right to supervise Congress and the Executive, let them do their jobs without judicial hectoring. It should protect basic citizen rights, but only if the Congress has seriously violated one.

"What rights, and how would the courts protect them?"

"Right to life, to begin with. Then there's your right of conscience, which I think is what the First Amendment is really all about. You have a right to your opinion, especially on matters of public concern, and you have a right to express it without fear of punishment. There's a yawning gap between jailing someone for speaking up and for punishing them for spending more than the legal limit of their own money in running for Congress. The Court needs to respect that gap.

"You also have a right to a fair trial, done according to established principles of law and judicial practices to protect the rights of a citizen against arbitrary prosecution. Those are a starter. The Four Freedoms enunciated by Roosevelt might fall into a different category though still important."

"And how would the judiciary protect these?"

"Not by proclaiming a law unconstitutional but by refusing to hear a case that criminalizes one of these rights and by issuing a writ of habeas corpus on behalf of anyone unjustly jailed."

I nodded. "The court withholding a power properly belonging to it while not invading the proper domain of the other two branches. Neat," I said.

"You think?" she said.

"I think," I said.

By this time we had reached Great Falls.

"You know," she said, "this is only the second time I've been here in all my years in Washington."

"I biked out here a lot when I was living in DC. They closed the Parkway on Sunday so bikes could use it. I'd bike out to Great Falls and back, almost forty miles round trip."

"I always suspected you're a glutton for punishment," she said with a gentle laugh.

"Pure pleasure, believe me. In May, the Potomac, swollen by the spring rains, thunders down the Falls. It's something to see. Follow me."

I led the way to a building that had once been a tavern serving canal day trippers from the district, now a museum of the C&O Canal. We went down a small bank and out to a point of land facing the falls where I spread out the blanket I was carrying in a canvas tote bag.

"Let's sit," I said. We sat, the Falls not much more than fifty feet away, close enough to wet our faces with a light spray.

"Wow!" Carol exclaimed, taking a good look at the roaring turbulence that seemed to be rushing straight at us. "Stunning," she said breathlessly, "and scary, too."

We sat there silently for several minutes agog as the Potomac made its last tumultuous descent from the Appalachias.

Wow!" she said again."

I leaned over so our shoulders touched.

CHAPTER FOURTEEN

I always thought Congress could be a better job with the arrangements of its hearing rooms. The spaghetti jumble of cables for microphones and other electric devises for the media makes an unsightly mess before the witness table, made worse by the almost comical scrum of photographers squatting before the witness table. The chamber and the event deserved better.

I watched as Jessup McDowell took his seat, dressed in a dark blue suit with a noticeable pin stripe, fitting his slender body as though tailor made. It said big important law firm. The coterie of lawyers accompanying him were nearly as well draped. They were there to insure no question from the senators lured him into dangerous mine fields, legal or political. Carol did that kind of work, but she sat at the table with the witness, representing him.

The Chairman of the Judiciary Committee, Senator Jackson F Matthews, sat at the center of this somber array like the keystone of a dark suited arch. He was leaning over whispering something to Senator Malcolm Berger, the committee ranking member. Senator Berger was there to help Jessup McDowell navigate the choppy waters of the upcoming hearings over which dark clouds had already gathered. Many of the senators there, like Matthews, were skeptical of McDowell's candidacy, if not downright hostile to it.

Senator Matthews banged his gavel and began. He read a brief opening statement welcoming Jessup McDowell and stating why they were all there and moved straight into his first question, a prerogative of the chair.

"Mr McDowell, you have written extensively on the separation of powers. I've looked exhaustively through the Constitution and can't find the term there. Can you tell the committee what you mean by the term and how it applies to relations between this Congress and the Court to which you've been nominated?"

Jessup McDowell, slightly above medium height with the body of a serious jogger, looked ready for the committee, test him as it might. He was configured for combat, as the military sometimes puts it. He leaned slightly forward to tap his microphone.

His phalanx of supporting lawyers leaned forward, too, gripping their fully stuffed brief cases, ready with whispered advice, their tight, satisfied smiles smug with confidence.

"You are correct, Senator," his voice and body language showing accommodation, "the term is nowhere found in the founding document which binds us all."

Senator Matthews had made sure I had a good seat able to see and hear everything. If I were one of the his high priced legal guard dogs, I might have leaned forward at this point and warned Jessup McDowell against any high toned liberties with the good senator. Senator Matthews might come across as a simple Wyoming cattle rancher, but he was a master of Washington's labyrinthian ways, in an out. His down county appearance was just that, a facade. Inside he was shrewd and knowing.

This could be a long day, I said to myself with a smile.

"Then why do you use it? You seem to regard it as an undisputed constitutional principle, obvious to all."

"I use it," Senator, "he said with just a hint of patience, "because it is clear from the very structure of the government bequeathed us by our founding Fathers," tone here of Moses referring to the tablets of stone, "who created a separate legislature, a separate executive and a separate judiciary, each with its own defined powers. I think it a fair conclusion that each of the three branches is sovereign in its own domain, outside encroachment impermissible." He leaned back with a satisfied little smile.

"A common observation," the Senator said dryly, "but let me ask you this. What affect, if any, do Article I, Section 8, and Article III, Section 2 have on this Separation of Powers?"

"In Article I, I presume you are speaking of the power of Congress to institute courts inferior to the Supreme Court?"

"I am, yes"

"And in Article III, section 2, you are speaking of the Congress's power to make "exceptions" and "regulations" for the Court when acting in a appellate capacity?"

"I am."

"Well, all I can say is," here reminiscent of a law professor humoring a callow law student, "Article l refers to courts inferior to the Supreme Court, and Article lll refers to the Court only when it is acting as part of the appellate system. Neither Article touches the Supreme Court as created by Article lll, Sections 1 and 2. I would think it above argument that what the Constitution has created is beyond the powers of Congress or the Executive to modify or reform."

"With certain reservations, I might agree. But save that for another day. Would you agree that Article l and lll do create a nexus between the Congress and the Supreme Court and all lower federal courts?"

"Administratively speaking, yes. I agree, the Congress has the power to confirm judges, set the number of justices to sit on the Supreme court and to create the entire federal court system inferior to the Supreme Court. But it has no power to interfere with the Court or the courts in the administration of justice. That must be free from outside, I mean political, interference. Justice must be blind to all considerations except the facts and the law."

"No disagreement there. And that is not the area of my concern. No one in this Congress to my knowledge would dream of compromising the integrity of our courts, including the Supreme Court, in the rendering of justice. We have no intention in removing Lady Justice's blind fold. But you are aware, I am sure, that there is a public perception that some justices have received lavish gifts in the form of vacations, plane travel and other considerations from donors, almost all very wealthy, who have or could easily have business before the Court. Most of these gifts have not been reported as required by current law on the grounds they weren't really gifts. There is a public concern this creates favoritism in the Court's rendering of decisions. There are pubic calls for Congress to establish a code of ethics for the justices of the Supreme Court similar to the code in effect for all other federal justices. If this doesn't compromise the integrity of the lower courts, why would it compromise the Supreme Court?"

"I agree, the code now in effect in the lower courts does not compromise their integrity. That isn't the issue. Congress created the lower courts and can clearly create a code of ethics for them as long as it does not impinge on their power to render justice. But it did not create the Supreme Court. The Constitution did, and it created the office of justice of the Supreme Court with a lifetime tenure as it created the power of original jurisdiction. If Congress cannot add to the Court's original jurisdiction, how can it impose a code of ethics that would meet constitutional scrutiny?"

His coterie of lawyers leaned back with satisfied smiles.

"Because we have the power to name the number of justices, to name where and when they will sit, and what other responsibilities they may have and to agree to their appointment to the Court. Let me remind you that until the end of the nineteenth century, Supreme Court justices were required by Congressional legislation to ride circuit, serve as justices in lower federal district courts. The practice is not mentioned in the Constitution, but Congress's right to impose it has never been disputed. If we can do all that, I find it hard to believe we can't impose a code of ethics on the Justices of the Supreme Court."

The smiles of his legal team drooped just a bit.

"I believe it is a matter best left to the Court," Jessup McDowell said.

"My time is up," Senator Matthews said with obvious regret. "I yield to the ranking member.

"Mister Jessup," Senator Berger said, "I want to thank you for your service to the American people and to the cause of justice. You spent several years in the Department of Justice as well as ten years on the federal bench in the Fifth District, isn't that so?"

"It is indeed, Senator, and they are among the proudest years of my life."

"As well they should be," the Senator said. "You left the bench to take a job with Schneider, Sikking and Noman, a leading Washington firm some seven years ago, isn't that right?"

"It is," Senator."

"And why was that? Why did you leave the bench to practice private law?"

"Senator, it was with deep regret that I left the bench. I have six children, three of whom are in college and three of whom are close behind. The salary of a federal judge is not enough to cover the heavy educational expenses involved." He paused for a moment, and then with a wry smile said, "Let me add, just in passing, this has led me to give serious consideration to public funding for all education."

Here chuckles from his legal team and an amused ripple through the crowd.

THE COURT

"But I gather even in private practice you did not totally abandon the public sphere. What was your focus in private practice?"

"I concentrated on cases protecting citizen's First Amendment rights in the practice of religion. There is a strong godless element abroad in the land that would circumscribe the practice of religion and largely ban it from public spaces. I defended those who insisted their right to practice the religion of their choice is unassailable and beyond the each of a faithless government."

"And a noble cause it is, sir. But let me ask you, so there is no misunderstanding here, despite your sincere belief, you would not let your private religious views influence your judicial thinking in any case involving religion that came before you on the bench. Isn't that so?"

"That is so, senator, and I thank you for allowing me to make that clear. I would apply the law as written and promulgated, not my personal views, which remain mine and private."

"One final question, Mr McDowell. In all your years of public service in the Department of Justice and on the federal bench there has never been even a hint of scandal or suspicion that you ever took gifts (here the senator made air quotation marks) in return for favors. Am I correct in that?"

"You are, Senator, there is none. I would not demean myself by such contemptible behavior. I guide my public life by my oath to support the Constitution and I lead my private life according to the dictates of God."

"Quite right, the Senator said."

It was Senator Mike Andrews turn next, an ally of Senator Matthews.

"As far as I am aware, no one, certainly on this side of the aisle, has ever raised a suspicion about your personal integrity. If all were as you are perhaps a code of judicial ethics for federal judges, including those on the Supreme Court, might not be so pressing. As James Madison once famously said, if all men were angels, we would not need government. Unfortunately, most of us live somewhere between Hades and Heaven. The recent history of the Court more than bears this out. However, my good colleague and the chair of this committee has more than adequately addressed the issue. It is clear Congress has the Constitutional power to mandate a code of ethics for all federal judges, including those on the highest court in the land. However, there is..."

Jessup McDowell leaned forward to put is face close to the mic. "If you will excuse the interruption, Senator, I believe that is still an open question that might have to be litigated."

"There is no open question in our mind. The only issue is whether it is better to let the Court take the initiative or have Congress do so. The American people have waited patiently for the Court to see the obvious and act. I remind you, justices are not some form of heavenly visitor, with us but not of us, sent like the angels of the Old Testament by God to offer divine commands and heavenly instruction. It would be wrong for us to interfere with the courts as they dispense justice, but We the People have a right to demand of those dispensing justice, it be done with integrity. We the People must be confident justice is being done fairly and not in favor of some rich donor or another. We can impeach for bad behavior, and if that power is to mean anything, it must be based on clearly defined and well understood standards of bad behavior. An ethics code would be a step in that direction.

However, as I was about to say, there is another question on which I'd like to have your views."

Jessup McDowell leaned forward again, anticipating the senator's question, a gladiator ready to parry the next thrust.

"Mr McDowell, the judiciary and its advocates make much of the power of judicial review. They assert the Constitution as a written document has to be interpreted, and the agency to do that is the judiciary. Mr. McDowell, can you give me the Constitutional basis for that assertion?"

A small smile crept across McDowell's face, indicating he had easily detected the little trap the senator was laying for him.

"Well, of course Senator, there is no explicit provision in our founding document, authorizing a court to declare a government act in violation of the Constitution, as has been so often, and so tiresomely, in my humble view, pointed out. However, it is in the very nature of a court, just as armed violence is in the very nature of an army. No written constitutional provision is needed to tell the army it can use its weapon to defend the country, and there needs be no explicit provision to say a Court can compare a law to the written provisions of the Constitution and decide if the two are in accord or not."

He leaned back with a satisfied smile, confident the trap evaded. His legal team exchanged knowing little nudges.

"Yes, that's all very clear," Senator Andrews agreed, "courts are there to settle disputes according to objective, dispassionate criteria. It's an instructive analogy, but I'm not sure it's a complete one. The Court has often overturned legislation passed by Congress, even when Congress was using one of its designated powers. I give you a case of some years back in which a wealthy man running for the US Senate challenged a law that limited what he could spend of his own money to run for federal office. It violated his First Amendment rights, he argued, even though the law did not prevent him from speaking out against the law or urging its repeal. It just said there was to limit to what he could spend of his own dollars on his campaign, done to reduce the baneful effects of money in our elections."

"Yes, I recall the case, Senator. I believe the Court was correct. Protecting a citizen's right to speech, especially in the political context, is important enough to override most other considerations. Speech would have to pose a serious threat to public order before it could be curbed. Revealing military plans leading to military disaster for the nation would be an instance, what Justice Holmes once called a clear and present danger. The right to speech is essential to our political culture and should be given wide latitude.

"Protecting free speech is important, I agree. But here's the problem. Should all forms of speech, wherever, whenever and in whatever mode be equally protected, or is the essence of the amendment protection of our right to express our beliefs, opinions, and observations free of retribution? Aren't the means by which we express those ideas just that, means, not the right itself?"

"The Court has held it is that and more. Burning the flag in protest of a government policy or spending as much of your own money as you wish in furthering your candidacy for federal office has been held by the Court to be protected speech."

"I'm not sure I agree. To take another example, the right to speak out against union representation of government employees is one thing, but claiming exception from paying a fee for negotiated benefits you enjoy because of your political differences with the union seems a stretch. After all, those refusing to pay on grounds of principle don't reject the benefits on grounds of principle. By that same argument, couldn't you withhold taxes from a government with which you disagree?

"Some might want to make such a distinction, I suppose," Jessup McDowell said with studied patience, "but the Court has ruled that the First Amendment right is to be protected no matter if it's an expression of opinion or forced association with an organization you disagree with. To admit exceptions is to endanger the right, unraveling it step by step until it is entirely gone like a sweater being pulled apart strand by strand."

"A clever analogy but like all analogies they limp at some point. The essential point in effective governance is often the choice between a lesser or greater good. The Court's answer, as you articulate it, is that a right is a right and should be subject to no compromise, except in very extraordinary circumstances. Congress, on the other hand, if I might be allowed to speak on behalf of the entire body, faces a choice between goods, choosing the one that does the greatest good.

"There are no absolutes in real life and no absolute rights, including the right to life or to freedom. You can lose your freedom by violating the rights of others, and you can be forced to expose your life to moral danger in military service to protect the life of the society at large.

"It is the same with the First Amendment. Society needs to be free to limit the amount of an individuals personal funds spent in running for federal office as long as your right to speak against the law is not punished. Likewise, you should in good conscience be asked to help defray the cost of securing benefits you enjoy even if you disagree with the politics of the union securing them. You are not made to be in the union or pay full union fees, just a smaller sum to defray the costs of the negotiations on your behalf.

"To argue as the Court argues is an arid intellectual exercise doing nothing to solve the important, practical needs of the community. The constitutional principle cited is almost always one that leads to the political resolution agreeable to five justices. The Congress, in these two instances, chose to circumscribe in a small nonthreatening way the exercise of the First Amendment, in one instance to control the corrupting influence of money in elections, and in the other to secure a citizen's right to unionize, even citizens who are government employees. What are dry, abstract arguable legal principles in comparison to that?"

"All I can say, Senator, the Court, in its infinite wisdom, sees the matter in a different way. It is guided by principle, and nothing but principle, Constitutional principle, in its decisions, not pragmatic matters or political horse trading which too often can lead to the violation of an important principle."

The rest of the day proceeded in similar fashion with Senator Matthews and his forces questioning the public utility of judicial review and Senator Malcolm Berger's side defending it as a matter of principle.

CHAPTER FIFTEEN

"You make a nice fire," Carol said snuggling closer on the couch facing my fire place.

The first cool nights of Fall were upon us making a fire a welcome thing. Carol came over to help me inaugurate the season. She brought a big bowl of first-rate chili. If she wasn't a lawyer, she could have made it as a chef. I supplied the rest, a nice apple crisp for dessert, a robust California red to make it all go down easy, and the fire.

"Learned it from my dad. We had a fireplace, and dad was very particular about building a fire. We had a lot of apple wood from a nearby orchard that had been bulldozed. He said the hard apple wood made the best fire, and the smell was good. We first made a bed of kindling in the form of a rick, laid on top of that two medium sized logs and then one large one on top of those. He then crumpled up a newspaper page and shoved it under the rick, sparked it up and sat back to watch the flames slowly grow in the kindling, reach up to the medium logs, get them going and finally watch as they engulfed the big log. It always seemed to me the flames were like fingers reaching up to the open sky above the chimney. It was almost as good as watching TV."

"Sounds like a good dad," she said.

"I have no complaints. He often used such moments to teach. When he took pains to get the nest of kindling right he'd say, good big things come from good little things."

She laughed appreciatively. "I see some of that in you."

"I'm flattered. When I look back on it, it seemed he was laying down little buoys to help me avoid the shallows.

She laughed some more. "You seem to come by your gift of expression honestly."

I nodded happily. This was snuggling as it should be. If this was it, no more, I'd still feel perfectly content. Time with Carol was time well spent. But often snuggling was just the entry point to more intense stuff. We were getting good at it.

"A phrase you used in your piece about the first Jessup hearings struck me."

"Which phrase was that."

"You said, judicial review often seemed like exercises in judicial theology."

"Yeah, it does."

"How so?"

"The Court treats the Constitution as a biblical text of which they, the high priests, are sole explicators."

"Yeah, fair, at least somewhat. What's the alternative? I'm just being devil's advocate; I'm not really arguing with you."

"Cases come to the Court by way of a complaint that a law or action by the executive has caused injury to someone's interest, as you well know. Let's say Congress passes a law stating certain states with dubious records of civil rights must vet changes to their electoral laws through the Department of Justice. A state objects to the "unfair" singling out, and argues further things have changed from the bad old days, the law is based on outdated information, superannuated.

"The Court agreed and nullified that part of the law. The Constitutional principle? None I know of forbidding a burden placed on one state but not on all, or that Congress must use the most recent information in making its laws. The Court may think Congress sloppy in its procedures and inconsiderate of the feelings of some states, but those are not against the Constitution. It seems the Court had its own view of federalism, personal rather than rooted in the Constitution. It just didn't like what the Congress did and came up with some specious Constitutional argument to stop it. Is that really its business? And keep in mind, after that decision certain states began passing all kinds of voting restrictions aimed at targeted groups. The bad old times were over?"

"Okay so far. I'm familiar with the case."

"And?"

"I'm not going to say. I want to hear what you have to say first. Let's say the complaint might have some merit. What's the affected state to do, just sit back and take it?"

"Why go to the court? Why not take your complaint to Congress, who can fix it, if needed?"

She looked at me.

"Citizens, and states, have a right to petition Congress for a redress of grievances. Moreover, each state has a congressional delegation to argue its case."

"So, then, why go to court?"

"Short answer, a better hope of prevailing there than in Congress. Choose the right lawyers and your chances improve of winning five judges over. Lot easier than trying to get a congress that has already spoken on the matter to change its mind."

"Something I know a little bit about," she said. "There is such a thing as judge shopping."

"Right, and not helpful to the democratic processes. Going to court atrophies our political muscles. In this instance the Court said Congress had the right to pass such a law but didn't pass it in a good way, not in keeping with the Constitution as read by them. In other words, you have a right to do what you did, but we don't like the way you did it. The Constitution, the Court said, enshrines certain values of fairness which you have violated.

"Question: is a judgement such as that not better left to the voters who have a direct interest in the question rather than to judges whose reading of the Constitution might be idiosyncratic, not widely shared by the public? Are we talking principle, or best practice? Was the Court exercising a preference for states rights over federal rights? Is that it's business? What's more important for the public good, fair voting laws, or that some state doesn't feel slighted? There is the sense in cases like this the Court has an agenda which it uses due process or the first amendment read in a particular way to secure. Too often it under cuts Congresses use of its Article I powers."

"So you're saying in effect the better avenue to settle such disputes is the political rather than the judicial."

"I guess that is what I'm saying."

At that point we stopped talking and let the fire entrance us into more interesting territory which we found in bed.

The next day I continued my comments on the Jessup hearings.

I wrote, "The assertion is the Supreme Court defends the Constitution and protects the rights of the People. The Jessup hearings are telling a different story. The Court uses the Constitution as a way to dip its oar in the political waters.

It was different in our earlier years. The Marshall Court confined itself to addressing relations between the states and the federal government. In one case it stopped Maryland from taxing a federal institution, a branch of the Bank of the United States in Baltimore. In another, it stopped New York from granting a ferry monopoly between Manhattan and New Jersey, that violated the Commerce clause of Article I.

"Things changed at Dred Scot. Politics entered the Court's proceedings. The South, seeing its power in the Senate wane by the addition of new non slave states, wanted the slave issue taken from the political arena. The Court, using the due process clause of the Fifth Amendment, complied. It overturned the North West Ordinance, which had barred slavery from territory north of the Ohio river and east of the Mississippi, and then overturned the Missouri Compromise, which forbade slavery from territories north of Missouri. The Congress, the Court said, could not take a citizen's property- slaves-without due process, presumably some kind of court proceeding. So the South was free to take slavery anywhere it wished in territories not yet states, the issue now beyond politics.

"And civil war came.

"The judges arguable Constitutional readings take precedence over preserving the peace of the nation.

"Dred Scot was overturned by the Civil War and the subsequent 13th and 14th Amendments, strong indications the "People" did not want what the Court said it should have.

"Even so, the Court continued to use the Fifth's due process clause to keep wayward legislatures, national and state, in line. It slapped down those Midwestern states who tried to keep predatory railroads from fleecing their farmers. Railroads were private property, the Court said, wagging its finger, and their profits could not be seized without due process, a clear defense of big money against little money.

"The property the Fifth Amendment referred was more like private homes, personal goods and papers, the kind of things arbitrarily seized by crown authorities from fractious colonists. It does not mean large, semi public economic enterprises which unregulated can wreak great economic or social damage. The Court conveniently ignores the difference between Mr. Rockefeller's private home and his vast oil empire. One is protected, the other needs government oversight.

"Taking the Court's broader view of property rights the Court eviscerates so much of the Constitution's Article

I. Surely this is not what the Constitution had in mind. The founders weren't all that unmindful.

"The mindset, government is Constitutionally prevented from regulating the economy without the Court's permission, straddled the 19th and 20th centuries. New York state legislated a limit to the number of hours bakers could be made to work, a health measure. The Court said no. The state could not preempt the workers "right" to bargain for their hours, so what if individual workers were in a poor position bargaining against management's concentrated power. Unions would rectify matters. The Court took a dim view them as well, holding unions would "monopolize" labor, interfering with the right of contract between workers and employers.

"During the Great Depression, Congress in the National Recovery Act gave the president the tools he needed to pull the economy back from the abyss. The Court stopped it, protecting Constitutional principle. 'No' it declared, 'Congress could not delegate these powers to the executive, even in a national crisis. Business's right to keep making the kind of disastrous mistakes that brought on the Depression must be preserved. It was in the Constitution.

"Yet the last paragraph of Article I, Section 8 of the Constitution, saying Congress can "...make all laws... necessary and proper for carrying into execution the forgoing powers..." gave Congress all the leeway and flexibility it needed to solve the nation's knottiest problem, until the Court got in the way.

"In the Court's view, Constitutional purity must prevail over the government's ability to respond to the people's needs.

THE COURT

"It drove Roosevelt to try to pack the Court.

"There are times, as I examine the history of the Court, it seems the Justices believe the real America is corporate America, created by and protected by the Constitution.

"We will have more to say on this theme as the hearings progress."

CHAPTER SIXTEEN

"You don't have to do this, you know."

I looked at her. "I want to do it." I hoped she wouldn't ask why.

"I appreciate it," she said quietly.

Her doctor was in Frederick, a forty-minute drive. She could drive, it wasn't that. She had been noticeably tired these last few weeks, even in bed. In the past when she really wasn't up for it, she would still try to please me. These last few weeks I sensed it was becoming an effort. Then I would just hold her tight.

She was in with the doctor close to half an hour. I idly leafed through the stack of magazines that was standard in every doctor's office. I tried not to let my thoughts run wild. When she finally came out, I looked closely at her face. Her face always told you what was going on with Carol. I saw concern and determination.

"Let's get a cup of coffee," she said. She had something to tell me.

THE COURT

The Whole Bean is a trendy coffee shop on the banks of the stream marking one end of old town Frederick. It has outdoor tables for those who want sunshine and a burbling stream. We stayed indoors.

Carol came to the point, as she always did.

"I have leukemia," she said flatly. No drama, no pathos. Just the fact.

I tried not to let my jaw drop. This was a time to stay strong.

She read the look in my face.

"No, no," she said quickly, "it's treatable, the doctor said."

I relaxed, just a little. Treatable? So's pneumonia, until it's not.

She told me what the doctor said. "He said I have Chronic lymphocytic leukemia, the most common form among adults."

"Treatable? Chemo?"

"Yes. He's setting it up now. He said we've caught it early, and the prognosis is good."

"And you'll get better? All the way better?"

She laughed. Was I being silly? This all seemed too serious for joking.

"What he says. The chemo works in a majority of cases like mine."

The hearings resumed after a long weekend, made longer by our trip to the doctor and Carol's news.

The usual parties were in place, the curved bank of senators, whispering to one another or shuffling papers, the witness, alone in gray charcoal pin stripped splendor at the witness table, his bank of advisors settling themselves for the grim day ahead, and we, the audience.

The day would be grim for the nominee for sure, the tone set by the first day's hearing in no danger of changing.

Senator Matthews banged the gavel, and the day began. The questioning had gone the entire arc of senators and was once more back to him.

"Mr Jessup', he began, "I want to continue exploring with you the civic utility of the Supreme Court."

"Senator?" Jessup McDowell said acidly, eyebrows arching at the impertinence of the question.

"The Court's civic utility, Mr McDowell," Senator Matthews repeated a little impatiently. "The Court is created by We the People. We need to see if we are getting what we bargained for, delivering justice and protecting the rights of the People."

"The Court is there to exercise the jurisdictions given it by Article 3 of the Constitution. Is there a claim it has not done so?"

"No," said the Senator, "no problem there. It's how the jurisdiction is used that concerns us. The Preamble to the Constitution says the Constitution is enacted to establish justice, promote the general welfare and secure the blessings of liberty, among other goals. So let's examine a couple of cases to see how they stack up against that criteria."

Jessup McDowell stirred nervously in his seat.

"Let's take all these Second Amendment cases that have so roiled our politics recently and incited so many of the mass shootings we've suffered through. It would be fair to say the Court has eviscerated state and local authorities' power to protect their people against gun violence.

The People have an intrinsic right to own weapons almost without restraint, according to the Court, the right infringed only under the most extraordinary circumstances. The result, authorities can protect us against mayhem on the roads and violence from abroad but not against domestic gun violence."

"I don't think it is fair to blame our mass shootings on the Court, Senator," Malcolm Jessup said dryly.

"Really, Mr Jessup? When a municipality tried to curb the use of large capacity handguns they were told only if there was already a historic precedent for such restrictions. Check history first, it was told. If history offered no precedent, a new one could not be created. It didn't seem to matter that such handguns did not exist back then. How has this principle advanced public safety?"

"I think that's also unfair, Senator. The Court is simply applying the law, in this case the Second Amendment, which clearly says, and I quote," he said, glancing down at a paper, '.. the right of the people to keep and bear Arms, shall not be infringed.' Even a layman can understand that."

"You left out the preceding clause which says "A well regulated militia, being necessary to the security of a free state..." Doesn't that suggest a citizen's right to bear arms was conditioned by the need for a militia whose ranks were filled by private citizens who supplied their own arms, muskets in those days. The Minute men of Revolutionary War fame? The amendment was meant to protect a state's ability to raise a militia when needed, not to protect an indiscriminate right to own guns of whatever kind. Applied literally today, it would mean private citizens could own

F-16s, Abrams tanks and so many other modern weapons not even conceived of when that amendment was written.

"We no longer have militias. They are replaced by the National Guard, armed, as you know, by the federal government. The 2nd Amendment is made redundant by these developments. Times change and the Constitution, must change with them, if it is to have any relevance today. In 1789 an armed citizenry was a necessity because of frontier troubles, lack of a police force, still unsettled relations with our former master, Great Britain, internal uprisings, problems that largely don't exist today. An armed citizenry is no longer needed. Its place has been taken by the police, the national guard, and the Department of Defense. Private citizens toting military weapons like the AR-15s are more a public hazard than a public protection. The Court's highly particular granting of an abstract right to bear arms does nothing to promote public safety.
"The Court didn't see it that way. It takes the citizen friendly view that citizens have an Constitutional right to own guns, militia or not."

That's a highly individualistic reading of the 2nd Amendment. Reading it as a generic right to bear arms is a perversion, and in any case who is better suited to make that decision, the Court or an elected legislature?

"All I can say, Senator, the Court is dealing with eternal Constitutional principles, not shifting political needs. There is the amendment process."

"Yes, but it's slow and uncertain. Should public safety be forced to rely on such an uncertain process? The often rapidly changing needs of a modern society require something more expeditious."

"I'm not sure what you mean."

"Maybe my meaning will become clearer as we move on. Let's examine the case in which the Court ruled corporations are people, permitted to make donations to political causes the way any citizen can. It loosed a flood of dark money into our elections.

"People, of course, come about by biological procreation, their rights intrinsic. Corporations are created by government charter, their rights derived from those charters. There are no universal charter rights as there are universal human rights. What is the Court's authority to give corporations a right not contained in its charter? Isn't this a political issue?"

"Senator, I wasn't on the Court at that time and can't be expected to answer for it. I'm sure, though, it had good solid legal reasons for what it did."

"Constitutional reasons? Or perhaps an agenda supporting the monied interests' desire to dump buckets of money into our political processes to secure influence? Doesn't this decision better belong to Congress than the Court? If Governments create corporations, shouldn't it be government that decide what rights they have? Why does the Court presume to interfere? Our legislatures make the law, not the courts."

"Well, Senator, obviously the Court has not seen it that way. One of its functions is to say what the law is. What more can I say?"

"Not much, but we, the Congress can and will. It is my intention to propose reforms of our federal court system, including the Supreme Court. We want the courts to apply the law, not make it. The Court is not a body derived from some Platonic juridical ideal, abiding with us but not of us, its powers intrinsic, not from the Constitution, its pronouncements definitive and eternal. Am I being unfair?"

"Perhaps a bit dramatic, Senator."

CHAPTER SEVENTEEN

Carol's first Chemo session was at one, plenty of time to make an easy drive to Frederick. She hated early morning appointments. Her mornings always started with a hearty breakfast, and she didn't like being rushed.

The long, rectangular room was lined on two sides with large, well padded chairs that could be tilted far enough back to allow sleep. Beside each chair was a upright stand on dollies for drip bags. Slightly more than half the seats were occupied by patients, all hooked up to the bag hanging next to their chairs. Some patients were covered with blankets and a few wore soft wool caps, presumably to cover the hair loss from the chemo. Besides each chair was a smaller one for anyone accompanying the patient.

I was glad no one asked my relationship with Carol: family, guardian, care giver, what? I didn't have an easy answer. I wasn't family, a guardian or professional care giver, and I wasn't sure how far friend or friend/lover might fly.

Happily, no one seemed to care. If Carol wanted me there, it was good enough for them.

And she did want me there.

There wasn't anyone else, in any case. Carol was not the kind to collect friends. She had many acquaintances, warm and friendly as she was, but her few close friends lived in DC. To be close to Carol took something special.

Fortunately, I had it, whatever that is. I suppose it's what made me approach her that first day at Patty's Patio, and drew us closer the more we were together. We grew, we didn't just connect.

I was with her at the clinic because it was important to me to be there, not just to show support but because she had entered my inner fortress, the way family can. What threatened her, threatened me. She wanted me there. She didn't say that, just conveyed it by little looks and gestures.

The leukemia hadn't bitten all that deep and she looked slightly out of place among the other patients some of whom were clearly in advanced stages of the deadly killer. Some apparently were unable to get to their chairs without help. Carol could on her own steam. I was there not because the leukemia had disabled her but because she was a part of me.

She was hooked up to her drip and the process of killing her cancerous white cells began, the causes of the leukemia. Her healthy white cells needed to be secure from the cancerous ones so they could continue to keep protecting her against infection, their main job. But chemo would weaken her immune system in the meantime and we needed to be careful about unnecessary exposure. That would be my job. Carol was going to be safe.

THE COURT

Once the tube was in her arm she leaned back to get comfortable.

"You bring a book?" she asked. I hated dead time, sitting there with nothing to occupy myself. At a doctor's office or restaurant before the food came, wherever I had to wait, I made sure I had a book with me.

"No, I thought we'd just talk." I never brought a book when I was with her.

She glanced quickly at her neighbors. "The way we talk?" she said quietly. "Might upset some of the neighbors." She laughed.

We talked about all kinds of stuff, the way intimates do, mundane and not so mundane. But our serious talk was about politics in its many forms. Both of our professional lives revolved around what the government was up to and all the currents public and private that moved the sea weed in our political waters. We both had well developed, well informed opinions and were as likely as not to say something that might upset a casual hearer who didn't share our politics.

So we just chatted about trivia though it wasn't our strong suit. Occasionally she leaned back and closed her eyes.

'You need anything?" I asked the first time.

"No, just taking a breather," she said. "I'm keeping score," she laughed
"So far it's chemo 50, cancer cells 0." She laughed. Dark clouds held no fear for her.

It was over soon, and she was unhooked. We left for The Whole Bean, becoming a habit. As soon as we were there she said, "So what do you think will happen with Jessup's hearings?"

"Senator Matthews and the Democrats on the committee are pushing an agenda, hard. They mean to reform the federal judiciary, Supreme Court most of all."

"My impression, too, just from reading the reports. Not sure about some of it."

"Which part?"

"No particular part at the moment. I'm just wondering how far they intend to go. I don't want the Court totally under the thumb of Congress. I agree, it's made some really questionable decisions, and they use certain provisions of the document as a means to play politics. I get all that. And I also agree that as the creator of the federal courts, save for the Supreme Court's original jurisdiction, Congress has the right to impose reforms. I'm curious to see what he has in mind."

"If I know Senator Matthews, whatever it is will be thoughtful."

"How do you feel? I asked. This was her first chemo.

"I feel with my hands," she said laughing and then shaking her head at the silly joke. "Sorry," she said, it's the medicine they're shooting into me, makes me a little drunk. How do I feel? Too early, can't tell. I'm imagining the battle going on inside me between the medicine and the cancerous white cells like these medieval paintings of battles, opposing forces decked out in armor, on horses and swinging big swords or charging with long lances, the medicine taking on the bad white cells like the Guelphs and the Ghibillines."

"The what?" I said, laughing. Is this drunk Carol or intellectual savant Carol?

THE COURT

The Guelphs and the Ghibillines , two political factions in 12th century Germany and Italy, one, the Guelphs, supporting the Holy
Roman Emperor, and the Ghibillines supporting the Papacy. The issue dividing them was the right to appoint bishops and abbots in Germany and Italy, an important political question in those days. The Guelphs supported the Emperor's power to make those appointment, the Ghibillines sided with the pope."

"So that's what's going on inside you, the Guelphs and the Ghibillines punching it out?" I didn't know to laugh or not.

"Metaphorically," she said with a grin.

"So who won, the Guelphs or the Ghibillines?"

"It dragged on until the 14th century when the papacy finally got the upper hand."

"I'm remembering now something about Todi, that town in Umbria?"

"Yeah, I remember, the truffle sauce."

"Well, something else. The city still has good parts of its medieval walls, and the merlons, those small stone dividers on the top of the wall, were swallow tailed. Other cities they're just flat topped. I Asked somebody about it. Swallow tail, I was told, signaled a Guelph loyalty, the emperor, the flat tops, Ghibillines, the Pope. Something like a flag. So your cancer cells, Guelphs or Ghibillines, who's winning?" I wasn't sure how far she wanted to go with this.

"Oh, Guelphs for sure. The temporal power should rule, not the church."

We left it at that.

CHAPTER EIGHTEEN

"It's clear now where the McDowell hearings are headed," I wrote, "major court reform. Congress, led by the Democrats, is tired of the Court playing politics, acting as the complaint bureau for the moneyed interests.

Does the Court even have such a right? We will come back to this point in a future column.

"At the moment the committee, in the person of its chairman, Senator Matthews, is asking the Court to show how its legal machinations advance the general welfare.

"Dred Scot took the slavery issue out of politics, where it properly belonged, and plunked it down in the court house, where it didn't, to be frozen beyond further discussion and possible solution.

"In the Granger cases already cited state legislatures trying to protect their farmers against predatory railroads were slapped down by the Court, protecting the big railroads against the small farmers. Later when NY limited the number of working hours of bakers could be made to work in a day, the Court again stepped in to protect the "right" of bakers to bargain for their hours, forgetting individual workers had poor leverage against the owners with their concentrated power. No matter, a "Constitutional" principle was at stake.

"Allowing the law to stand would have given the bakers safe working hours without reducing the bakery's profit by any significant amount. Shouldn't an elected legislature be free to make such adjustment without the interference of an unelected Court? Which did the general welfare the most good, the Court' solution or the legislature's?

"The same question could be put to limiting what an individual can spend of his own funds to run for Congress. Allowing the wealthy to spend what they want in running for office expanded the corrosive effects of money in an election. What suited better the public need for fair elections, the restraints imposed by Congress or the lack of restraint allowed by the Court?

Treating corporations as people also opened the flood gates to large streams of dark money in our elections. Again the common good sought by Congress or the arid judicial solution of the Court?

"All this using of the 1st and 5th Amendments to undermine the Congressional exercise of its Article I rights is what, a defense of the Constitution or the Court playing politics? Who would blame a sceptic for thinking the real right being protected is the right of big money?"

CHAPTER NINETEEN

Carol was now several weeks into her chemo treatment and the Guelphs seemed to be winning. There had been an apparent set back a few weeks earlier when her doctor said he wasn't satisfied with her blood work, a more extreme treatment might be in order. I feared she would lose her hair and become extremely feeble as so many patients seem to.

"What would you do if I lost my hair," she asked.

I prized her long, tawny tresses, loved running my hands through them at certain exciting moments The loss, even temporary, would be painful.

"Buy you a wig?" I ventured.

"How about a nice cap or hat instead?"

"If that happens, I'm going to sue your doctor. Know a good lawyer?"

She looked at me.

But it was a false alarm. Either her body had executed a miraculous turn around, or the blood work was misleading. After her most recent chemo, her doctor gave her a thumbs up. The cancerous white cells were rapidly diminishing.

Her doctor was a replant from India and spoke with the distinctive Indian sing song version of English. He was a kindly man and gentle. You could see right away why he was a doctor. He was truly concerned about you. "Well how are you today, you are looking very well," was his invariable greeting, not the professional greeting of a doctor's practiced manner, but the real thing, his eyes gleaming with genuine concern, shining on me as much as on Carol, his gentle gaze searching your face, looking for the good.

Carol and I both let out a sigh of relief.

"Hold the wig," she said to me.

I was heartened enough by the news to ask her if she'd be up for a concert at Kennedy Center.

"Sure," she said brightly. "What are we hearing?"

"The National Symphony Orchestra," I said.

"I guessed that," she said, "I know your tastes. What are they playing?"

"A new piece just commissioned by the orchestra, a piano concerto by Mozart and a symphony by Tchaikovsky."

"Wow, Mozart and Tchaikovsky on the same bill?"

"You know classical music?"

"I played French horn in high school. Yeah, I know something about it."

"You're like an onion," I said with a happy laugh.

She gave me a look? Not a peach?

"The more you're peeled, the better you get."

She laughed. "Okay," she said, "I guess."

"I had no idea you played an instrument," I said, "let alone a French horn."

"Why? What've you got against a French horn?"

"Nothing. Just if I had to guess I'd say piano, or maybe guitar. Seems what most people would do."

"My parents weren't most people. French horn is cheaper than a piano and everybody plays the guitar, even those who can't."

I laughed.

"What's so funny?

"I just realized now why it is you pucker up so good." I ducked, afraid she might throw something.

"You have no idea," she said with a tight little smile.

I decided to drive to the Kennedy Center rather than take the Metro. Traffic is lighter on Saturday evening, there is no Metro stop convenient to the Center, and the Center has parking.

I picked up the 270 at the Darnestown interchange, then the Beltway to the GW Parkway, the most direct way to the Center.

"So how far does Senator Matthew intend to go with his reforms?" she asked. "I'm still a little uncomfortable about judicial independence."

"If you knew Senator Matthews, you wouldn't be," I said.

"That's reassuring," she said. "The chatter in some legal circles is not. Senator Matthews is seen there as a traitor, attacking a sacred American institution."

"Over done," I said, "he has no intention of turning the Court into an adjunct of the Congress or violating Lady

THE COURT

Justice. He simply wants to stop the Court second guessing the Congress on matters in its purview. There's a difference between protecting the basic rights of a citizen and putting a particular spin on one or another feature of the Constitution to enact the Court's view of a political issue. The Court is there to apply the law in disputes not make it or change it. It has no place being a political player."

"And yet," she said, so much of the legal profession, most particularly judges, think just that, they are political players protecting eternal Constitutional values."

"Yeah, "I said with a laugh, "as they see them."

The concert met expectations. The clean but quietly elegant, near utilitarian lines of the concert hall made a clear contrast to the Baroque splendors of Rome and other European venues I knew during my sojourn in the Eternal City some years ago. The less decorated lines of the Kennedy Center concert hall say New World. Occasionally I miss the baronial richness of the European concert halls, a type speaking of power and elegance that have little to do with the performance on stage, more about the stature and wealth of the hall's builder than art.

You could present Mozart in a barn and it would still be art of a level and richness rarely seen in this world, aristocratic venue or not. Mozart's music is aristocratic, but it's the aristocracy of art not of politics or pretentious worldly splendor.

His piano concerto was the second item of the concert. The first piece was a work recently commissioned by the National Symphony. The composer was on hand to take a bow on stage following the performance, a youngish woman in a long gown that I guess was making some kind of aesthetic statement. She took her bows to warm applause, the audience showing its appreciation for what it has just heard and encouraging her to go out and do it again.

The orchestra sat on their chairs looking out at the audience or practicing snatches of the piece to come as the stage managers moved front chairs around and rolled out the concert grand for Mozart's Piano Concerto number 24 n C minor.

The soloist was a young Polish pianist of glittering reputation named Stefan, his last name too littered with consonants for easy pronunciation. No matter, he gave a lively and beautifully sculpted performance of Mozart's mosaic like colors and graceful melodies weaving through the movement in sinuous, delightful guises.

Carol had wondered about Mozart and Tchaikovsky sharing the same bill, an unusual occurrence. Both are headliners, and some would consider it bad concert hall manners to ask two such equal luminaries to share the same stage. But there was a certain musical logic to the program. Tchaikovsky deeply admired the music of Mozart, valuing it far more than Beethoven's. Though there are few surface resemblances between the music of the two masters, the way their themes journey through a movement deftly changing colors and dramatic modes shows a deeper affinity. Perhaps it helps to remember that Mozart was a master of the operatic stage and Tchaikovsky strode the world of ballet colossus-like. Both use drama and directness of expression to reach their audiences.

THE COURT

The National Symphony under a conductor who knew and loved the music did more than justice to both composers, After, as I walked up the aisle, I felt even better than when I arrived, my happy anticipations more than fulfilled. I glanced at Carol walking beside me. How had she taken it? She looked quietly content, thoughtful, a good sign.

As we made our way up 270 back to our rural sanctuaries I asked, "Did you enjoy it?"

She remained thoughtful for several long seconds as though asking herself if she enjoyed it or not. Finally, she said, "I'd have to say yes. This may surprise you, but this is the first classical music concert I've ever attended. I wasn't sure what to expect. I thought it might all be a little mysterious and beyond me."

"And?"

"Well, no, I did enjoy it, though I'm not sure I can tell you what it was I was enjoying. I mean it's not like a Rock concert, you can say I liked this song or that song and everyone pretty much knows what you mean, maybe not why you liked it but at least what you liked. Here there was so much music, rich and extended without break over a long period of time. Parts of it I liked a lot, more than some other parts, especially when I thought I could hear a melody."

"What would you say the difference is between Mozart and Tchaikovsky?"

"Tchaikovsky was louder, more forceful, with more flashing lights than Mozart."

"And Mozart?"

"Lively, graceful?"

"Good for a first time," I said.

"I knew you liked it, so I was going to take it seriously, not just go through the motions."

"I'm flattered."

She smiled. "You should be. But tell me something, what's this C minor stuff all about. I'm not quite ignorant enough to think the term means the same as it does referring to a person. But what's it mean that Mozart's concerto is in C Minor"

"It's what they call a key signature."

"I know that," she said. "The French Horn, remember?"

"I'm no musician and can't give you a technical answer, or even on technically informed one," I said. "But take the octave in musical notation?"

"Yeah," she said, voice leaning forward, "the notes go from A to G, do, re, me, fa, si, la di, do?"

"Yeah, that's it. As I understand it a key is simply the arrangement of steps between the notes. Going from do to re is a whole step."

"Mmmm," she said, "I remember that."

"But every whole step is divided in two, the black keys on the piano. You can play several notes at the same time, all ten, to make a chord. If its all whole steps it's one key, a combination of whole and half steps makes another key, each key its own combination of whole and half steps.

"OK."

"So the best way to look at what keys mean to the music is to look at them the way a painter looks at colors. The whole steps, prime colors, the half steps shades of a prime color, the various combinations giving the overall tone the composer is looking for.

"So one key is all prime colors, another would be a shade of that color, major and minor?"

"Yeah, something like that, "I said.

She laughed.

"What?"

"Can't wait until the next cocktail party so I can drop that on somebody."

"Yeah, and them watch them walk away shaking their head."

"Would depend on the cocktail party." She remained silent for a bit, mulling it all over. Then she asked, "You know a lot about Mozart?"

"I love his piano concertos. I'm even able to sing some of the melodies which makes me feel close to Mozart. Unlike Beethoven, who strikes me as craggy and too much into himself, Mozart is someone I would have enjoyed meeting. According to contemporary accounts, he was fun at parties, loved puns and pranks, had a potty mouth-to put it no deeper than that-and all in all could be good company. He also had to have had a deep if somewhat melancholic understanding of human nature, especially women. It is said his arias for the female characters of his operas are the equivalent of vibrant, probing character sketches.

"Yeah, sounds like my kind of guy, too."

Many of them are among the most perfect music ever written, in my opinion. And I'm not the only one. Beethoven thought so, too. There's a story I read somewhere about this concerto. It's only one of two Mozart wrote in a minor key. I don't know why that's important, but apparently it is. Beethoven, it is said, played this piece in concerts and is said to have been impressed by a section of the last movement that shifts gracefully from the minor to the major as though Mozart intended to finish the piece in a grand, heroic romp in the major, but then deftly and gracefully shifts back into the minor to finish in a equally grand conclusion in the original minor mode. Beethoven is said to have sighed at this musical magic, "we shall never see its like again."

Brahms was familiar with the story and remarked that Beethoven tried to replicate the moment in his own Third Piano Concerto, also in C minor. But, according to Brahms, Mozart remained the master of such graceful musical legerdemain.

"You could use that at a cocktail party, too."

"You laughing at me?"

"No. I like it when you talk this way. Just don't want you to get too heavy, too serious. I prefer happy conversation to seminars."

"Noted," I said.

That night we made sweet love. We were growing happy together. It was also a sign the leukemia was slowly losing its grip on her.

CHAPTER TWENTY

Editorial meeting at the Standard. The Standard, that is us on the editorial board, had a number of pieces out on reform of our federal system. We were going all out, no holding back. The idea was to set off a hot discussion of our federal system, where it was strong and where it needed to be shored up. There was a lot of the latter.

How we conduct our federal elections was one big area. Collectively, Bob Suggs covering Congress, our editor, Jim McMahon, Steve Archibald, on the executive branch, me covering the Court and Leroy Swan surveying the states had contributed articles on the question of elections and representation.

In sum, our position was this: democratic governments govern with the consent of the governed, that is we select the people we want to make the decisions, the laws, that will govern us. Elections are the life blood of a democracy, and our system is healthiest when elections are as unfettered, clear and comprehensive as possible, allowing all voices to be heard equally well. Any restrictions or clotting of the process is as harmful to the body politic as sclerosis is to the body biologic.

Our examination of how we work our elections shows the US has a poor circulatory system.

For starters, there is the egregious electoral college which seriously distorts the popular vote. It must be abolished.

Then there are the distortions of Gerrymandering, chopping up and rearranging the electoral map to advantage one party over another, candidates choosing voters rather than voters choosing candidates.

There is the mal representation between rural and urban votes making a farmer's vote more consequential than a city dweller's in state elections, done to insure "pure" country values prevail over "corrupt" urban ones.

There is the squeezed choice of our single member, first past the post of Congressional House elections often throwing up victors who often have only tepid support.

There are the various political devices such as picture ID requirements, the old literacy tests, restricted number of voting places- most located in favored areas-inconvenient elections days, all sorts of practices to muffle the popular voice rather than clarifying it.

And finally there is the electoral monstrosity of the US Senate in which populous California has the same voice as near empty Wyoming or Idaho. The country's population is so badly represented in the US Senate that a numerical minority of Senators representing more than fifty percent of the US population can be outvoted by a numerical majority representing less that fifty percent. There is a historical reason for this, but it has long since lost its validity, yet it remains with us like the traffic laws of the horse and buggy era.

There are cures for these many and various ills, and the Standard has proposed several of them over the past many months. Multi member Congressional districts with rank ordered voting is one, eliminating Gerrymandering and making more likely the election of candidates with the widest support through combining first and second choice ballots. It also improves the field for third parties widening and deepening the varieties of the public voice.

Making a state's senate delegation reflect the size of its population is another. Some even advocate changing the Senate from a legislative body to an upper legislative consultative chamber, a sort of senior advisory board for the Congress, representing not states but regions organized along coherent geographical, historical and economic lines.

And these are just a start. Our Constitution was written partly in reaction to the excesses of the British Empire and to the chaos of thirteen newly independent states squabbling like unhappy inheritors. It may have met the needs of 18th century America, but it doesn't satisfy the requirements of its 21st century descendent with its highly developed economy and multi racial society whose politics and culture span a continent. If it did, we would have universal health care, a fully representative government and a president elected by popular vote. We don't. We need reform.

CHAPTER TWENTY-ONE

The McDowell hearings have concluded and the Senate Judiciary Committee is now chewing over what it has heard. My private view is McDowell has at best a fifty-fifty chance of winning nomination. His view of the Court as pope to the bishops of the executive and legislative branches is not what the committee and Senate want to hear.

"Reform is in the air, and it is not in the direction of an autonomous court dictating to the rest of the government. There is a growing feeling on both the Hill and Pennsylvania Avenue that the Constitution is not the private preserve of the Court; it belongs to the People whose representatives in both the Congress and the White House can best apply its provisions to solving the nations political, economic and social problems, the country ruled by political processes, not judicial ones. The Court is there to apply the laws, not make them.

Senator Matthews' questioning the civic utility of some of the Court's decisions tells me both McDowell and the Court are facing some rough weather. Accordingly, in preparation for what is coming I offer the following observations for our readers.

"The Justices, misleadingly citing John Marshall make the Court the constitutional conscience of the nation, its declarations the last word on the constitution.

"This position has no constitutional basis.

"The Constitution says almost nothing about the composition and functions of the federal courts beyond defining the Supreme Court's original jurisdiction, a narrow lane confined to matters arising between two states-Ohio suing Kentucky over the location of their boundary in the Ohio River-or involving foreign officials on US soil. Beyond that, the Supreme Court is the last link in the chain of federal appellate courts, subject to whatever "exceptions" and "regulations" Congress imposes.

"Judicial Review is a job unique to the Court, so it says. That begs as many questions as it answers. Is the Constitution a legal document in the same way a contract or an ordinary law is, or is it the founding organ of government laying out its powers and institutions?

"What does unconstitutional mean? There is no definition in the document itself. If Congress is using one of its Constitutional powers with implications, significant or not, for another part of the Constitution, does that make the act unconstitutional? In Dred Scot and the Granger cases, the Court used the 5th Amendment's due process clause to override Congress's exercise of powers under Article 4, Section 3. Is the Constitution so rife with inner contradictions it cannot function without being vetted by the Court?

"This is what the framers intended?

"Who is the best judge of the constitutionality of congressional or presidential acts, a court or the voters who elect them? Who says if a measure is constitutional or not? Is it a legal question or a political one? The document offers strong suggestions. The voters can throw out members who have violated the Constitution of We the People, and the president can with the veto, though this is a partial power since Congress can overturn it. There is no mention of the Court's ability to nullify either acts or legislation. The ultimate meaning of the Constitution seems to rest with We the People, its meaning political, not legal.

"Answering questions about a disputed provision of a contract or law is a matter of civic practicality, if not justice, and is a proper function of a court. But does the Constitution have to be read all one way or all another? Can't there be a number of different ways Congress can use one of its powers to respond to a complex situation facing the nation? And isn't how the Congress uses its power best left to the judgement of the voters who have to live with the consequences? The lack of any specific method to overturn a constitutionally passed law other than by the citizen with his vote or the president with his veto suggests the framers thought so.

"An important justice agreed. Justice Learned Hand of the Federal District Court of New York, the country's most eminent jurist never to sit on the Supreme Court, said the ballot box, not the courthouse, was the place to settle challenges to a law.

"Marshall, the so called "founder" of judicial review, seemed to think that as well. Despite his assertion judges say what the law is, he never once overturned a piece of

Congressional legislation. Apparently if it was okay with the People, it was okay with him.

"And why should a judge, even a chief justice, give himself a power not given by the Constitution? No other part of the government can do that. The Constitution gives the Court no power to overturn legislation but it does give Congress the power to define the Court's jurisdiction. If there is such a thing as an unexpressed but assumed power, the advantage lie with the Congress not the Court."

CHAPTER TWENTY-TWO

Her doctor kept giving Carol good news. "You are looking very well," he said in his flavored English, meant as both personal compliment and judgement on her chemotherapy.

There were times as I sat beside her in that room of cancer victims, suffering evident in their haggard faces, Carol seemed in the wrong place. She didn't look like them, and I feared resentment on their part for being shown up by her more robust health. I knew better, as did her doctor.

Her condition, if left to its own devices, would have eaten her up inch by inch until the current stopped and her light went out, consumed by the ravenous cancer. It made me realize how precious she was to me and how threatened that was by this unhappy stroke of nature seeking to snatch her away. We were spared all that by the lifesaving skills of her doctor, so far proving more than equal to the disease. All praise to him coupled with my good thanks for letting me keep her.

THE COURT

Caught early was the big difference between Carol and her companions in suffering, stopped before it could clamp down fully on her. Otherwise, she would be at one with them in shared misery. Instead, she was well on her way to full recovery, as were many of them were, as well, though by longer voyage.

As I sat there, I felt lucky. This was not the sad end to one of the best things that has ever happened to me, only a severe rocking of an otherwise blest voyage, one I wanted to keep going. Feeling such relief and joy, I impulsively reached over and squeeze her hand.

She glanced at me. "What?" her look said.

"Just so happy this is going well," I explained.

She smiled. "Imagine how I feel," she said.

Shortly, the nurse came to unhook her, offering a complicit smile. "You are really doing well," she said.

In no time, Carol and I were at our usual table at the Whole Bean grinning across the table at each other like kids playing hookey. In silent celebration, each of us was having a nice Danish from the Whole Bean's rich offerings.

"You really threw the gauntlet down in your last column," she said. "Neither you nor the Standard are pulling punches."

"No, we're in it for the long haul. I'm puzzled why Congress lets the Court's mess around in its business. Why does every political dispute have to be a court case? I suppose one answer is so many members of Congress are lawyers, most of whom have an exaggerated respect for the courts, falsely assuming since they have the final word in criminal and civil trials they should also have the deciding voice in settling political disputes, falsely dressed up as legal questions.

"Yeah," she said, "but remember before Dred Scot the Court never challenged a Congressional act, yet there were probably as many lawyers in Congress then as there are now. Dred Scot, as you said, was the first time the Court declared an act unconstitutional, the first in a sorry line of such declarations."

"You think that?" I asked, hoping I was hearing right.

She grinned. "You can be very persuasive," she said. "Yeah, I've come around to the view that the Court is out of its lane in declaring an act unconstitutional."

"I'm flattered," I said with genuine sincerity, knowing she wasn't saying that just to please me. "Anyway," I said, "to continue my thought, Marshall, despite his beatification as Father of Judicial review, never presumed to overturn a Congressional law. He said a part of the Judicial Act of 1789 couldn't apply to him, but otherwise a law would have to be so egregious a violation of the Constitution it would be clear to everyone, no dispute. Otherwise, to use Oliver Wendell Holmes take on the question, judges shouldn't overturn a law just because they think it's stupid, wrong headed or contrary to their political philosophy. None of that makes it unconstitutional.

"And I have another thought on the question."

"Mmmm?" she said.

"It wasn't until the Gilded Age when big business, playing king of the national hill, felt the need to protect its pile against government regulation. The Court happily obliged by defining Free Enterprise as a Constitutionally protected principle.

"The legislatures are better at realizing the goals set out in the Preamble to the Constitution than the Court, that's your point?

I laughed. "I couldn't put it better myself."

She smiled. "As I said, I'm beginning to see things your way. Never thought about it much before, concentrating on the trees rather than the forest, I guess. But now that the point has been raised, I see the concern."

" It's not going to cut into your business, clipping the Court's wings?" I asked, teasing.

"No. You're after judicial review of Congressional legislation. There's plenty of business without that. Real legal issues"

"Something else has occurred to me," I said.

"What's that?"

"As I said, why does every Constitutional issue have to be a court case?"

"How else would you do it? I'm talking like a lawyer now."

"I repeat, if you disagree with a law, take your case to Congress, not the courts. As long as the Congress has followed the rules and is using a Constitutional power, the disagreement is political, not Constitutional. The Constitution is broadly written and should be approached that way, everything permitted except those things expressly forbidden. The Court, to give itself leverage, often reads it very narrowly or uses one section to over rule action in another. Congress has a right to regulate federal elections. That gives it the power to lay down the conditions under which elections are held, including the role of money. How this might impinge your First Amendment rights is as much a political question as it is a legal one. Freedom of speech is not the creature of the courts, it's the creature of the People. It was they through the amendment process that passed the First Amendment. There is no clear definition of what speech means, but certainly at its most basic level it must mean the right to express your private beliefs, especially on matters of public importance, free from retaliation. Beyond that, it's up for discussion. Why should a court be any better at that than citizens themselves or their representatives? After all, they are the ones who have to live with it, not the courts. The Congressional limit of how much of your private fortune you could spend to get yourself elected to federal office applies to everybody. It doesn't restrict what you can or can't say in your campaign, it just defines the conditions under which you can say it, essentially no different than imposing limits to how long you can take in addressing a Congressional committee on the issue, how much advertising space you buy up to freeze out your opponents, or so many other real life restrictions to insure fairness in elections. These are better matters of discussion and compromise than of a judicial application of an abstract principle that ignores real life consequences."

"OK, I can see the merits of that. But what if these discussions result in a decision to legitimize Communism?"

"Yeah, so? Belief in Communism or Socialism is not forbidden by the Constitution. It's a First Amendment Right. If a majority wants either one, how can any court stop it, and if a majority doesn't want it, how can any court impose it? In the Gilded Age, the Court held Free Market principles were rooted in the Constitution, government had to keep its hands off big business, not regulate it except in severe national need, no matter the distress caused the rest of society. Nobody accepts that anymore. Free Market principles are like any other political philosophy, open for discussion, the community free to accept or reject them. Why should the Court have anything to say about it? I know I've said this before, but it's important. We the People need to be governed by ourselves through our elected representatives, not by unelected judges, good as they may be at the law. We the People make the laws, not the courts."

She laughed. "That's a mouthful," she said, "and I wish I could argue with you, but I agree."

"And let me repeat, why do Constitutional issues have to be solved by the courts? Courts are not mediators or negotiators; they decide questions of guilt or innocence or right and wrong according to clearly established standards."

"Fair enough. But then who decides if a state statute violates the federal constitution or not?

"Why not Congress? It can form a special committee to insure accordance between state laws and the Constitution."

"Isn't that making the Congress, a party in the dispute, also the judge? Is that fair? Just saying."

"Not really," I said, "a court proceeding isn't the only way to settle differences. We don't conduct most public business that way, including legislating. Take the case in which New York state permitted a private company to monopolize the ferry service between Manhattan and New Jersey. New Jersey complained this violates their right to licence ferry services between New Jersey and Manhattan, and it violates the Constitution which reserves the regulation of interstate commerce to the Congress. The matter is clear and Congress tells New York to desist."

"So what happens if New York tells Congress shove it?" she asked

"What happens if it says the same thing to the Court?" I asked back."Jackson said exactly that to Marshall after declaring Jackson's desire to relocate the Cherokee nation from Geogia to the Oklahoma Territory a breach of the a treaty with the Cherokee."

"What happened to Jackson?"

"Nothing," I said with a laugh. "He moved the Cherokee to Oklahoma, anyway. The famous Trail of Tears? Marshall may have fumed, but he could do nothing but look on."

"And if New York said that to Congress?" I'm playing devil advocate again," she said.

"Congress has all kinds of ways of retaliating. It can withhold funds for federal projects in New York harbor, for example, even limit the activities of the state's congressional members under the powers of section 4 of Article 1. And I'm sure there are any number of other ways Congress can compel compliance. When whisky distillers in western Pennsylvania refused to pay a federal whiskey tax, Washington sent out the army to quell the rebellion and collect the tax."

"I vaguely remember that from my history classes," she said. "So what happened?"

"The distillers got the message and payed the tax, and Washington called the army back."

"Oh, right. I remember now. So your point is Congress is more effective in enforcing its edicts than the Court. All the Court has is respect for the law. Lose that and it is powerless. Congress has real muscle."

"Yup."

By this time the Whole Bean was filling up with the lunch crowd and our waiter was anxiously eyeing our table. A line was forming at the door. The message was, please order lunch or free the table. I read her glance. "Time to go?" I said to Carol.

She looked around. "Yeah", she said, "looks like it. How about a walk on the tow path?"

"Excellent idea," I said, "let's do it." It was an encouraging sign. Her health was making a rapid come back.

CHAPTER TWENTY-THREE

"The Senate Judiciary Committee has finally spoken, and with a thunderclap. It has denied Jessup McDowell's candidacy and is revealing the outlines of court reforms it wants Congress to adopt. No more legislators in judicial robes, its says. Constitutional questions will be settled by means other than judicial trial.

"It limits judicial tenure to sixteen years after which Supreme Court judges remain on the court at full salary but no longer fully participating members with a vote. They will be judges emeritus, available for judicial firemen assignments on lower courts of appeal, as special masters or other judicial assignments by the Chief Justice. This will allow each president a nomination to the court and will infuse fresh blood periodically into the Court's proceedings. It will not require a constitutional amendment; it lies within Article I powers of the Congress.

"The federal court's jurisdiction to decide the constitutionality of congressional legislation will be limited

THE COURT

to obvious violations of the Bill of Rights which criminalize protected rights. Laws affecting rights but not nullifying them or limiting them in an essential way shall not be judicable. The People have a right to keep important government secrets or protect itself against calls for the violent overthrow of its government. Restrictions short of these are to be challenged at the ballot box not the courthouse. In the rare instances of deciding the constitutionality of a law or an executive act, the vote on the Supreme Court will be 6 to 9 and can be overturned by a majority vote plus five in Congress. This will insure the People have the final word on how they are to be governed, as Lincoln put it after Dred Scot

Carol proposed another of her Italian meals but this time at my place. "Can't beat that fireplace of yours," she said. She just brought all the ingredients and made herself at home in my kitchen. She was carrying a large canvas tote bag.

"What's in that?" I asked, idly. All her food ingredients were in large plastic containers.

"You'll see," she said, the teasing another sign the old Carol was making a fast comeback. "You have a good fire going?"

That was a hint. "Been going about an hour," I said. "I'm beginning to suspect something."

She grinned. "Thought you might. A good bed of hot coals will be nice."

"Because you're going to...? I glanced at the canvas tote bag.

"Right," she said, pulling out two small wire tripods and a long spit. "A nice piece of meat roasted over the fire," she announced proudly.

"That Italian lady taught you well," I said. "Really good Italian country restaurants cook their meats on a grill over an open fire. The flavor is so much better."

"Hope so," he said. "This is my first try at this. Can't tell you how hard it was finding the right tools."

"For sure. Roasting over a fire is no longer the American way," I said.

"One more casualty of modernity," she said.

"Defeated by you," I said. "I'll set it up while you do the rest. What's the meat?"

"Pork. Couldn't find a small suckling pig, but the pork shoulder will be a nice substitute."

"Super," I said. I set up the tri pods each side of the fire and skewered the pork shoulder and set it on the stands. There was a crooked handle for turning the roast. The heat quickly embraced the pork and sent a fetching aroma wafting through the room.

"Nice," she called from the kitchen, "starting to smell like supper." It took little time to finish her kitchen preparations, and the roast was starting to brown when she came out to join me, carrying two glasses of wine. She handed me one. We settled together on the couch to admire the roast, take in its aroma and watch it drop sizzling splashes on the fire.

"What else we having?" I asked. "Black truffle sauce?" I asked eagerly.

She shook her head, making my hopes droop. Not some garden variety tomato sauce, I hoped. Carol wouldn't do that when it could be something like black truffle sauce. She read my face and laughed, teasing me, almost a default mode with her.

"White truffle sauce," she said deadpan.

"Didn't know there was a white truffle," I said.

"See, you didn't learn everything there was to know about Italy when you were there."

"Guess not," I said, chastened. "Where'd you find them?"

"Same place I found the black truffles, a small grocery in Georgetown specializing in European delicacies."

I felt flattered. Truffles were not cheap in Italy. They didn't exactly grow on trees. In fact they grew under them, or at least near them, and were hard to find, almost impossible without a well-trained truffle hound. I could imagine what they cost here. Carol was not stinting.

"Can't wait," I said.

But wait we must. The roast would take at least another half hour or so before it was ready. I got up from the couch every five minutes or so to give it a turn.

We sat there for several long minutes before she said anything. I knew she was dying to talk about the Senate committee's recommendations on the Court.

Finally, she spoke. "You think it will fly, forcing justices to retire after sixteen years?"

"I think so. There is a gathering mood in the country that the Court is not the island it supposes in our national waters, sovereign in itself, answerable to no one. Besides, the justices aren't being forcibly retired, just reconfigured. They're still in the Court at the same salary so there's no violation of the Constitution. But after sixteen years they no longer have a vote and will hold themselves ready for any assignment the chief justice requires, except hearing Supreme Court cases, or at least deciding them.

"And Congress has the power to do this? What if the Court overturns it?"

"It won't because it won't be given the chance. The committee proposes denying jurisdiction to the federal courts over the law, which I'm sure you know they can do."

She nodded. "Remind me again why that is."

"Article l, section 8 empowers Congress to establish courts inferior to the Supreme Court and Article III, section 2 says when not exercising original jurisdiction the, which is confined to cases between states or involving foreign officials in US soil, it is the ultimate appeals court, "...with such Exceptions, and under such Regulations as the Congress shall make." In other words the Court when not exercising its original jurisdiction is the creature of Congress. Congress can assign or deny jurisdiction to any court, including the Supreme Court in its appellate configuration. Congress can affect the atmosphere in which justice is done as long as it doesn't interfere in the doing of justice. Anyone who denies that has not read the Constitution. The Constitution made Congress the boss over the judicial and executive branches. It hasn't always played that role, and it has certainly conceded way too much to the courts, allowing them to decide issues that really belong to the Congress, but it has the formal power to prevail. The only power that can fully correct Congress according to the Constitution is the voter, We the People."

By now the roast was ready. We sat at my dinning room table of Scandinavian design and enjoyed our ante pasta, pasta with white truffle sauce-an equal competitor to her black truffle sauce-roast pork, which really did taste extra good because it was cooked over an open fire, roasted potatoes and fava beans made in the Florentine way, all accompanied by a robust California red. We took our Grappa over to the couch and settled down to watch the fire.

"This might be a long slog," she said, "this reform."

"Could be," I said, "but you have to start somewhere. Our whole system needs review and reform. The Court is a good start."

She thought about that for a while and snuggled closer.

"Some meal," I said.

"Some fire," she answered.

THE END

www.ingramcontent.com/pod-product-compliance
Lightning Source LLC
LaVergne TN
LVHW020436070526
838199LV00063B/4758